ARIANNA

AND THE
SPANISH
SARDINES

J.B. CRAWFORD

ISBN: 1494221764

ISBN 13: 9781494221768

TABLE OF CONTENTS

CHAPTER 1
SAN TO TPA

Arianna Curtin picked up her shoulder bag and small backpack from the X-ray machine at the San Diego International Airport, SAN, visibly irritated at the shakedown of air travelers by the Transportation Safety Administration. She felt invaded, violated, all in reaction to the insane behavior of loony religious fanatics. She put her shoes back on, wondering how a terrorist could get enough explosive material into the heel of a shoe to destroy an airplane. So far, she was forced to produce her boarding pass and photo identification three times just to prove she was who she was.

"There needs to be a way for me to be seen as a loyal, native-born American, presenting no threat to public safety," she thought to herself. "Why can't they use facial identifiers, the computers that can read a person's features and verify who they are? They even have machines that can read the iris in a person's eye from yards away. They make me feel like a prime suspect in a vicious crime, a serial killer, an *unsub,* like on TV. I am so glad I was not forced to stand in that machine that looks through my clothes!"

"Ladies and gentlemen," the public address system came on, "announcing non-stop service to Tampa. We will begin boarding at this time. Those passengers requiring assistance may proceed to the boarding gate. Please have your boarding pass ready for the flight attendant."

Arianna watched as passengers began to stand, gather up carry-on baggage, get out boarding passes, and head over to the line forming to enter the aircraft. She was all ready, pass in hand. She gave it to the gate attendant who passed it quickly through a scanner and handed it back to her. She maneuvered down the aisle, checking row numbers, turning sideways to get around people placing luggage in the overhead compartments. She stowed her backpack then slid across two empty seats to the window on the left side of the airplane. She located the seat belt ends, clipped them together, and pulled the strap firmly across her lap.

The plane pulled away from the terminal and taxied out to the runway. "Ladies and gentlemen, this is the captain speaking. We have been cleared for takeoff and will be airborne momentarily." Arianna felt the release of the brakes and the increasing power of the jet engines. She was pulled firmly back in the seat by the thrust. The stubby light stanchions along the runway flashed by faster and faster and then seemed to drop away from the airplane as it lifted gracefully from the grasping earth and rose into the freedom of the sky. She watched as everything got smaller and smaller. The airplanes on the ground looked like toys. The houses and buildings were made for tiny dolls, not real people.

Arianna stared intently at the fading earth below. She saw a clear line separating San Diego from the deepening, darkening, vast, endless Pacific Ocean. To the north lay La Jolla and

Mission Bay. She could see the tip of Point Loma, the long expanse of San Diego Bay, Coronado Island, and the complex freeway network of I-5, I-8, I-15 and I-805. Sailboats tacked over the emerald green and power boats left straight white lines as they sped across the water. Arianna could hardly breathe, watching with excitement as the sea and land dropped further and further away and the aircraft made a slow turn over the ocean and came back toward the east. Further out, the ocean darkened and became a barren expanse while down below the land turned to a brownish blur. Clouds formed beneath the wings.

Arianna was on her way to DeSoto, the miniscule Florida fishing village where her mother grew up and her pioneer family had settled in the 1880s from Tangier Island, Virginia, in the middle of Chesapeake Bay. They made a living on Tangier Island gathering oysters and soft shell crabs to ship fresh and alive to Richmond, Baltimore, Philadelphia, New York, and Boston. Before Tangier Island, her people lived on the Cornish coast of England's southwest tip, even back then making a livelihood from the ocean as commercial fishermen. Nowadays, in DeSoto, her family continued to live the salt water life, mainly catching and selling blue crabs, stone crabs, red mullet roe, grouper, food shrimp and live bait shrimp, plus bait fish, notably Spanish sardines and thread herring used by sports fishermen to catch tarpon, sailfish, marlin, and other large trophy fish. This was her first trip to DeSoto, but felt in her heart that she was going home, entering on an adventure during spring break to visit her grandfather, B.D. Bradford, a commercial stone crabber in the old village.

Her excitement was due in large part to the stories she heard from her cousin, Nathan, who spent the previous Thanksgiving holiday in DeSoto. He shared with her his days on the Moondown with Cap'n B.D. Bradford, also known as *Pop,* their grandfather, hauling traps and bringing in stone crab claws. He told her about Pat and how the two of them found out the true meaning of friendship and, yes, real love. Nathan was ashamed of his thoughtless mistake in allowing a trap to knock Hands, the first mate, to the deck breaking his left arm and puncturing a lung. He was nearly in tears when he described the first aid he gave and how Hands was hoisted from the crab boat by a Coast Guard chopper and whisked off to Bayfront Medical Center in St. Petersburg. She could not wait to see Cousin Wally's dock, Nathan talked about so much. She was determined to eat raw oysters for the first time, and like them, even with Louisiana hot sauce. The single most important message Nathan passed along to Arianna was that DeSotoans, men and women, boys and girls, were special, sturdy, strong, able to meet any challenge, and had proven themselves in the village of DeSoto for over a hundred years to be self-reliant, independent, and capable of making their own way. Nathan announced with pride that their DeSoto forebears could make something out of nothing, spin straw into gold. "They helped make America great," he told Arianna, proudly.

Arianna's eyes blinked once quickly, then closed as sleep came.

"The captain has turned on the fasten seat belt sign. Please see that your tray tables are securely fastened and that all seats have been returned to their full, upright, and locked position. We will be landing in Tampa shortly. On behalf of the captain and crew, we appreciate your flying with us and hope your stay in Tampa is a pleasant one."

Arianna looked down at the pure white line of beach and the brilliant green of the Gulf of Mexico. Farther in from the long, straight, barrier islands, she could see the spreading expanse of Tampa Bay, crossed to the south by a very long bridge with bright yellow cables holding the center span high above the ship channel. She knew that had to be the Sunshine Skyway. Three long, flat causeways ran east-to-west below the airplane, connecting the beaches to the mainland over the shallows of Old Tampa Bay. Power boats left straight white lines as they sped across the water. MacDill Air Force Base covered the tip of the peninsula that jutted south into Tampa Bay. To the north of the downtown office buildings, she could make out a large football coliseum.

Thump! Arianna heard the wheels touch down on the concrete runway. She looked out the window to see the stubby light stanchions flashing by as the powerful reverse thrusters and hydraulic brakes slowed the giant aircraft. She was moved firmly forward in her seat by the deceleration. The stanchions flashed by slower as the airplane taxied to the terminal at Tampa International Airport, TPA.

CHAPTER 2
HOME TO DESOTO

Arianna passed through the igloo of the deplaning ramp. She looked out through the wall of glass and saw an elevated tram car approach the building. The doors to the tram slid silently open. As the passengers entered, the loudspeaker announced, "We are about to depart. Please stand clear and hold handrail." The tram glided smoothly and quietly out onto the elevated concrete track in the open air. Arianna was stunned by the bright, clear light.

"We are arriving at the landside terminal and airport hotel. Please exit through the doors indicated by the green flashing lights. Follow red or blue symbols down the elevators or escalator to baggage claim. Ground transportation is at all baggage claim areas," the well-modulated voice on the speaker said. She got off the tram inside the main terminal.

"Arianna, Arianna!"

She looked up and saw her grandfather, B. D. Bradford, waving at her. His skin was very dark, accenting his bushy eyebrows and his deep-set eyes. B.D. wrapped his big, brown arms around her, swept her up, and carried her away from the pressing crowd. Arianna felt the crush of the bear hug.

They walked together, Arianna stretching her stride to keep up with the elderly man's rigorous gait. They took the red elevator to the top floor of the building. The doors opened onto a glass enclosed area. As Arianna stepped out onto the roof parking lot, she felt the clear, clean, fresh April air.

"Florida weather is very close to perfect this time of year. You're used to more dry, desert air. There's a lot more humidity here than California. Come over here and take a look."

Arianna followed him to the parapet at the edge of the parking lot. From nine floors up, the flatness stretched away to the horizon. Water and land differed only in color, hardly in elevation. The low and featureless panorama accentuated the sky, filled with silver-blue, lazy, bulky, cumulus clouds. Everything felt clean.

"Look over here. That's Raymond James Stadium, home of the illustrious Tampa Bay Buccaneers." He leaned against the masonry wall and pointed. "Over there is the main part of St. Petersburg. You can see Tropicana Field where the Rays play baseball. That's Tampa Bay away over yonder." Arianna noted her grandfather's slow, rounded, drop the endings, cracker drawl. He said Flar-da instead of Flor-i-da. This land was different from California. Everything was so flat and there was water everywhere. The air was pure and easy to breathe. The light was bright and clear, the sky dominant.

"We'll be heading out along that road over there," B.D. pointed from the parking lot parapet. "Then across that long highway, the Howard Frankland Causeway past the other side of St. Pete, then over the Sunshine Skyway. It's a nice drive. You'll enjoy it. On the way, we'll stop at

Skyway Jack's for lunch. That's a real treat." He went to the passenger side of a shiny, dark blue truck and opened the door.

"This is the truck Nathan told me about! It's really old, but it looks like new."

"It's a 1939 Ford pickup, V8 engine, 85 horse-power, 21-bolt, flathead. I've always wanted a truck like this and when I saw it on eBay, I jumped on it. It has been a big job getting it back into condition, but really worth it. This truck was built in the year I was born. In a way, it is just like me. It had a good design from the start, had lots of use, and everything still works. I'm proud to drive it."

The truck was a faultless deep blue. The open pickup bed at the rear had side stakes to keep cargo from falling out. The high, narrow white wall tires were new. The spare with a shiny hub-cap was bolted to a rack on the passenger side of the body. There was a full running board on each side that a person could stand on. A blue Florida antique car license plate was mounted on the back bumper. It read, *39 Ford.*

"In many ways, it's simple compared to cars nowadays. You can see the whole motor and get at everything pretty easy with ordinary hand tools. It's not like modern cars with all the computers, gadgets, power-driven equipment for steering, brakes, air conditioning, and pollution control stuff. They never heard of a catalytic converter when this truck was built. It is hard to work on a car today without complex diagnostic computer equipment. All you need for this engine is a screwdriver, a pair of pliers, and good ears to hear it run." He opened the hood.

Arianna saw a tag hanging from the battery. It read, "Warning! 6 volt battery, positive ground."

"What's all this about?" she asked.

"In 1939, cars had 6-volt batteries with positive ground. Now cars are 12-volt with negative ground. I put the tag on there to let anyone working on the car know that it is from another generation and that certain precautions need to be taken. It would be very easy to destroy the entire electrical system with the wrong voltage and wrong ground. The 8 spark plug wires run from the cylinders to the distributor, that round, black housing mounted directly on the front of the motor, between it and the radiator. The distributor is attached directly to the cam and sends spark to the cylinders in a carefully timed sequence. There is no timing chain. It's easy to get to and simple to work on. This old jalopy consumes a lot of petroleum products – elbow grease and midnight oil."

From the driver's seat, B.D. said, "You will be driving this thing, so pay close attention. It's not anything like modern cars." He placed a very small key, teeth up, into a slot on the right side of the steering column and gave it a half turn back toward himself. With his thumb, he pushed a chrome lever to the left. "That's the ignition switch. Turns the engine on and off, too, not the key." He pulled the choke knob all the way out and pushed a small button on the left side of the dashboard. The engine started with a very smooth and powerful sound.

"Sometimes I think the V8 engine did more to boost the Ford Motor Company than the Model

T and the Model A put together," B.D. said to Arianna as he eased the choke down toward the dash. The gears ground when he put the truck in reverse to back up. "Watch the gears, darling. There's no synchromesh on this buggy. And watch the brakes, too. They are the first hydraulic brakes Ford used to replace mechanically activated brakes, but sometimes you think the hydraulic power is all in your right leg."

Arianna watched intently. She wanted to make sure she could drive it when she got the chance. Nathan told her how he messed up when he drove the truck, but finally got the hang of it. Arianna felt ready to drive the blue truck. She had just completed the 30-hour driver's education class as a 10th grader, then passed the traffic laws and road sign tests. She had a California provisional learner's permit. A museum piece like her grandfather's truck would be a challenge, especially with that old-fashioned stick shift. She would lord it over Nathan when she got back to California.

They went down the corkscrew ramp, paid for parking, and followed the signs to I-295

South. Arianna glanced around the truck cab. Everything looked new and had that new car smell. The seats and door panels had been newly upholstered and the floor mats looked original. The only thing that indicated the true age of the truck was the steering wheel which was cracked in places and worn smooth and shiny from long years of continuous use. The center of the steering wheel had an artfully-designed V8 emblem with the "8" superimposed on top of the "V".

B.D. noticed her admiring the emblem. "I'm sure you know that is the horn, but I'm just as sure you don't know that this is also the lights." Surrounding the V8 emblem was a thin, black ring with a small round button at the top. "This way to the right, parking lights. To the left, regular lights. The high beam, low beam switch is on the floor to the left of the clutch pedal."

"Whew," Arianna thought. "Cars have really changed over the years. I would never have found that light switch, much less figured how to start the engine."

"Air conditioning," B.D. whooped. He started cranking a knob in the center of the dash board.

The entire windshield slowly rose out and up and a rush of air entered the cab. He reached under the dash and pushed a lever. A vent popped up in front of the windshield and air flowed rapidly through the leg space under the dashboard. Arianna felt the clammy sweat on her body begin to dry and she thought about the originality and creativity of the engineers who designed these practical devices long before auto air conditioning became standard. The truck slowed and took an exit off I-295 South, then went west to US 19, then south to Skyway Jack's, with the giant white rooster out front..

They settled at a booth and ordered sweet iced tea from a waitress wearing a black tee shirt with two fried eggs strategically imprinted across the front. The lettering said *Delicious Fried Eggs at Skyway Jack's*. Arianna looked around the room at the homemade art work advertising various food items. Skyway Jack collected pigs and long overhead shelves were crammed with pigs of every sort brought in by customers over the years. The whiteboard had many dishes listed that she had never heard of such as Philadelphia Scrapple,

Old Navy smoked sausage, brains and eggs. B.D. said he usually gets the liver and onions for two reasons, "First, they do a fine job with it, and second I would never cook it for myself at home." Arianna was reluctant, but agreed to give it a try. When the plates came, she was surprised to see that the meal was really good, especially with the grilled onions and mashed potatoes and gravy. They drank sweet iced tea.

"I used to come here all the time. Years ago, the restaurant was a few miles south of here right on the water. Fishermen would show up at 5 and 6 in the morning, get hot coffee, a big southern breakfast with grits, then head out on the water. Some would be back in the early afternoon and chow down again. This was when the original two-lane Skyway was built. Jack was in business when the second twin two-lane Skyway was built alongside the first one. After the center span of the newer bridge was knocked down by a freighter in 1980, the state built the new Skyway with the yellow support cables. Eventually, they took out the center sections of the twin older bridges and left the north and south portions as world-class fishing piers. The state government tried to get rid of Jack when the approaches to the new Skyway virtually cut off access to his little greasy spoon down on the water. Tried to give him the boot. He fought back. Everybody around here was on his side, too, and he beat 'em. To make up for his loss, he ended up with this place, serving the same food with the waitresses all wearing fried egg tee shirts. Skyway Jack's is a special place and Jack is a local hero because he was pushed around by the big guys. He fought back and beat 'em. Jack won."

On the way out, B.D. bought Arianna a black tee shirt with fried eggs on the front. She tucked it into her shoulder bag.

The truck climbed steadily as it approached the center span of the modern Sunshine Skyway. It rose to a dizzying height, sufficient for large, oceangoing freighters to pass under. Arianna admired the long line of yellow cables in the center that held up the twin bridges, side by side.

B.D. was intentionally boisterous, "You know, out in San Francisco, they now call the Golden Gate Bridge the Sunshine Skyway of the West. Heh, heh!"

They drove south across DeSoto Bridge and turned right onto Manatee Avenue, passing through downtown Bradenton. They drove in silence until they reached Perico Island and could see the bridge ahead to Holmes Beach. On the right side of Manatee Avenue, B.D. pointed out Aram's Market which served as the neighborhood grocery store for DeSoto and picked up casual business from cars passing by on the way to the beaches on Anna Maria Island.

"I want you to meet Aram while you are here. He is a friend of everybody in the village. Came here from Lebanon years ago to start a new life in America. We need more people like Aram and Nancy, his wife."

They turned left on 127th Street West, passing Becky's Bait and Tackle on the right, then went over the humpback bridge, past the Crab Claw restaurant and pulled into the yard of B.D.'s historic house in the old fishing village of DeSoto.

CHAPTER 3
COFFEE ON THE STEPS

Before the antique wall clock in the living room struck 6 times, Arianna had been listening to the tick tock of the pendulum through the closed door. It was 3 in the morning on her body clock with the change between California and Florida. It was time to rise and shine. She got out of the huge bed and went to the window. Outside were three very large and old mango trees filling the side yard. She pulled on a pair of cutoff shorts and the Skyway Jack's tee shirt. Noticing the coffee smell, she went toward the kitchen. Through the screen door, she saw her grandfather sitting on the back steps. There was a mug next to the coffee pot in the kitchen. She filled it. She saw a coffee grinder and a can of coffee beans. She read Jamaican Blue Mountain.

"Mornin', Arianna."

"Good Morning, Grandpa."

"Call me Pop. That's what your mother does. She and her sister called me Pop since they were little."

"Yes, she does. She always talks about you as Pop, so Pop it is, Pop."

Sitting down on the back steps, Arianna edged her back against the aluminum railing on the far side and blew over the surface of the coffee. She took a sip. "Ooo, now that's a stout brew. I'm going to need some cream and sugar in this stuff."

"What? And ruin good coffee? Take it slow. Try to get the best out of a sip. It works. I buy beans from Columbia, Guatemala, Hawaii, Kenya and I grind each pot fresh. I like French roast, Vienna roast, German roast. I settled on this Jamaican Blue Mountain for now, but I always have an eye out for something special. Keep sipping and pay attention to the taste. Listen to what's in your mouth."

Arianna took another small sip and held it in her mouth. She listened. She heard the bitter taste and it stayed bitter. She went to the kitchen and added cream and sugar.

They were quiet. Arianna watched B.D. rest his chin on the edge of the mug, gripped in both hands, elbows on his knees. His deep-set eyes moved around the yard taking in the row of royal palms along the street, the old two-story frame Alvah Taylor house across the street, the house with the red brick chimney in the next lot, the long shed with four garage doors, the blue truck.

"I come out here most mornings before first light. Best part of the day. Man can get some good thinking in. Helps me understand things better. Helps get things organized. I just sit here, sip coffee, and figure out what I'm going to do that day, or that week, or next month. I try to come up with a better way to catch more crabs. Here I am matching wits with a bunch of primitive, prehistoric critters, and I found out they are smarter than I am. Stalking the wily stone crab, that's what I'm up to." He was lost in thought.

"I was born in this house," B.D. said after a period of silence, "and I have sat on these steps as long as I can remember. It is my favorite place in the whole world. Darling, I am very pleased you are here. This is the first chance you have had to learn anything about your mother's side of the family. I know she is out there in California, living in a large city, enjoying things we don't have here in a little village, but she is in the right place. We gave her a good foundation here in DeSoto. Now you have a chance to see for yourself what we really are, just like your cousin Nathan when he was here this past Thanksgiving. I'm proud to say we turned him into a fine DeSoto boy. He is back in La Crescenta teaching his mother to call grits *grits*, not polenta."

Arianna smiled at the grits reference. It was true. Her mother, Heidi, and her aunt, Andrea, always called grits *polenta*.

B.D. said, "Our people came here in the 1880s from Tangier Island, Virginia, out in the middle of the Chesapeake Bay. They were commercial fishermen - oystermen and soft shell blue crabbers. Before that, they worked the water on the

Cornish coast at the southwest tip of England. The Bradford family arrived in this area with six brothers and two sisters, William, Nathan, Sanders, Joe, Marvin, Sam, Nettie, and Martha. Nettie was my great grandmother, so she is your great-great-great grandmother. Nettie married a distant cousin named Bradford, also from Tangier Island, so I ended up with the old family name. Every time I think about those early pioneers I swell with pride. All they had was a dream to build a new life in Florida and they made something good and lasting out of that dream. They settled here on Perico Island and turned to mullet fishing to make ends meet. They built homes and raised families. I am the fourth generation, you are the sixth. We DeSotoans have a firm tradition of self-reliance and independence. Other young men and women from Tangier Island came to DeSoto through the years and there were several early settlers who came from the Canary Islands and from Cuba. One thing all these people had in common was a strong work ethic. No job was too hard for them. If they did not know how to do things, they figured it out. They were sturdy and hardy. They openly bragged, men and women, that they could outwork anybody. They were tough, too. No one in this entire area would mess with a DeSoto fisherman. I mean no one, not even the law."

Arianna took this in. She learned in school about the early settlers in America and realized, with some surprise and inner satisfaction, that her own family had been part of that history since the founding of the Republic, both in Virginia and in Florida. She suddenly realized that she was a continuation of that history.

"DeSoto has changed over the years," B.D. continued. "The Bradford brothers came first, living as bachelors until they could establish a homestead and be secure that they could earn a living from the water in this new place. They built temporary shelters, mostly sheds and lean-tos with canvas sailcloth over the top. They fished from skip jacks, sail boats with a center board that could be raised to pole across shallow bottom. They used seine, trammel, and gill nets to catch fish, mostly mullet, but other fish as well. Pompano was the all-time favorite because it brought in the highest price. They built net spreads over the water, which I remember from my own boyhood. The whole waterfront was nothing but netspreads where the fishermen soaked their cotton nets in lime water then hauled them up onto the spreads to dry. When synthetic fabrics came in, the fibers would not rot, so the nets were stored on the stern of the boats and covered with a tarp to keep out the sun. Ultra-violet light replaced rot and mildew as the enemy of the nets. The netspreads were torn down. When I was a boy about your age, my hands were burned, cracked, and dried after soaking the cotton nets in lime water and hauling them up onto the spreads.

"Once the men were settled and built real houses, they went back up to Tangier Island and loaded their families and personal goods onto large scows, stretching canvas for protection from the sun and rain. They did this in the summer when the weather was more predictable, and sailed away, towing the scows down the Atlantic Coast, around the tip of Florida, here to DeSoto. There were no roads back then, so everything came and went by water. Eventually, the run boat, steam-powered it was, started coming down from Tampa to bring ice, fishing supplies, and mail, then returning to the city with a big load of fish."

Arianna tried to envision the village without roads and cars, boats without motors, and life totally separated from the outside world except for the steam-powered run boat. There were no telephones, radios, televisions, no electricity, no indoor toilets, no running water, no schools, no hospitals.

"That must have been a very good life, back then, quiet, stable, secure," she said to her grandfather.

"That's true in many ways, but people have a habit of creating trouble. The greedier fishermen developed stop netting. At high tide, they put rows of nets across the mouths of bayous and enclosed water. When the tide went out, they scooped up huge amounts of fish, 30,000 to 40,000 pounds, and sorted them out at the dock, throwing out most of the catch as trash fish. It was an obvious waste and some felt it verged on criminal abuse of public resources. Joe Bradford, a trammel net fisherman, was extremely angry and spoke out against this practice. The stop netters tied sticks of dynamite to the end of a long poling oar and shoved it under his screened porch sleeping room in the dark of night. That was a deadly serious disagreement. The dynamite blew his bedroom apart and rousted the whole village. Good old Joe, out of bed and in the outhouse to relieve himself, was spared. Not long after, he moved back to Tangier Island. Those stop netters were too much for him. That house is still there, just beyond the place with the red chimney. If you go inside and know where to look, you can still see where the wood splintered. Good thing he had to go to the outhouse."

Arianna's neck crawled thinking about the intensity of people's feelings and actions when fundamental differences surfaced. "Dynamite!" she thought. "That's serious business."

"No matter how hard people try," B.D. continued, "disagreements arise and fester, setting up blood feuds, brother against brother, father against son, fisherman against fisherman. Life in the village continued all those years and on the surface, matters were settled and quiet. Beneath the surface, the cracks were widening. The earliest arrivals claimed and homesteaded all the waterfront property and soon used that advantage to open fishhouses. Resentments grew as fishermen felt that the fishhouse owners were in collusion to fix prices. Not a shred of evidence ever surfaced to support that claim, but once the rumor started, it never stopped, and the fishhouse owners became the enemy for the hotheads. The fishhouses carried their people like a company store. If a fisherman needed bunting, leads, corks, twine and rope to put nets together, the fishhouse ordered the material and paid for it in advance. As the fishermen brought in fish, a part of the catch was deducted and applied to this revolving credit arrangement. The system worked. Fishermen would have been hard put to generate the cash needed to improve their business and the fishhouses would not have made any money without the fish the independent boats brought in.

"Everyone was right, and everyone was wrong. Prices paid for fish were perceived, across-the-board, to be too low. The cost of materials, supplies, fuel, paint, everything needed to keep going, was too high. In the late 1940s and early 1950s, some of the more independent-minded captains formed a Fishermen's Union. They made up little burgees and flew them from their radio antennas. Another group created a fishermen's co-operative which they named the Co-0p, pronouncing it, for some unknown reason, as the Co-Hop. They bought and sold their own fish. The idea was worthy, but in the real world, the Co-Hop had to compete with long-standing alignments and allegiances. It fizzled and failed, but not for lack of enthusiasm and energy.

"One thing about fishing is that it is very objective. If you catch fish, you win. If you don't catch fish, you lose.

"Well," as B.D. stood up and stretched, "So much for your local economics and history lessons for today. De Soto is certainly not just a quaint little fishing village with white pelicans. Let's get to work."

CHAPTER 4
THE BUBBAS

B.D. went inside the house. Arianna looked around the yard, sipping the last of her coffee. She surveyed the four-door, tin-roofed shed, the shiny blue truck, stacks of crab traps, the Alvah Taylor house sheltered by silver palms.

"Hey, pimple-face, where'd you come from? Ain't seen you around here before."

Arianna looked over to see a barefoot boy about her age leaning against a royal palm, his arm extended out, fingers spread on the trunk, one foot lifted and positioned high up against the inside of his other leg, like a flamingo.

"Just arrived from California," she told him.

"You must be one of old man Bradford's carpet-bagging, scalawag grandkids. There was one here last Thanksgiving."

"That's right, Mr. Mighty Mouth. That was my cousin Nathan. And who might you be?"

"I'm Bubba One and I hate girls, especially snaggle-toothed, goober-lipped, stringy-haired, cross-eyed hyenas like you. You got a kisser like a hog fish. Wipe that yeller snot off'n your ugly face."

"And you got a big mouth," she mimicked his drawl, "that oughta be washed out with soap. I have a good mind to do just that right now."

"You and who else? I'll give you a fat lip and a bloody nose if you ever come near me. Just cause you're a sissy girl won't stop me. You and your kind ain't welcome here! The likes of you and your snooty, uppity friends can't come here from outside and sneer at us fishermen. We're just as good as you are."

Arianna sizzled as Bubba One marched away, chin thrust up defiantly.

B.D. came out of the house with two pairs of yellow knit gloves. "Here," he said as he reached a pair out to her. "They may be a bit large for you, but you'll need them to get those traps on the back of the truck." He pointed to a stack of wooden stone crab traps in the yard. He showed her how to put her fingers between the slats and lift the heavy traps.

"Bring 'em over here," he told her as he climbed onto the bed of the truck. "I'll stack 'em."

Arianna hoisted a trap. "Oof! What's in these things, anyway?"

"Concrete. The weight keeps the trap on the bottom. Otherwise, they'd float to the surface or get carried away by the tide."

"How much do they weigh?" She staggered with her load and set the trap down on the flat tailgate. B.D. placed it at the front of the truck bed.

"Oh, 40, maybe 50 pounds. After we build traps, we line them up in the fishhouse parking lot in rows on unrolled sheets of roofing paper, tar paper, back-to-back with the lids open. Everybody gets involved. The cement truck loads up wheelbarrows which are rolled between the lines of traps. Another guy scoops out cement from the wheelbarrow with a 5-gallon bucket and pours it into the trap. We work fast, so some get a heavy pour, some a light pour. Open up one of the traps," he said to her.

She turned the latches, raised the lid, and picked up the line and the orange buoy stored inside. She read *X4318* imbedded in the cement. "What's this?"

"That's my crab permit number. Every stone crabber gets a number that starts with X. Look at the bobber. See the X4318 burned into the plastic foam? We also have our own color. Mine's orange. That's so we can tell our traps from the others just by looking at the color of the bobber floating on the surface."

"Makes sense. What's a bobber?"

"That round thing you are holding in your hand. It has several names, buoy, float, cork, ball, marker, bobber."

"How did you get the number in the concrete? Use your finger?"

"Nope. After the cement is poured, another guy tamps the cement flat with a small square of plywood attached to a long 2 by 2. Then right behind him, another one uses a metal branding iron and presses the number into the soft, flattened mud." Arianna worked up a sweat carrying the heavy traps over to the truck.

"You drive!" B.D. tossed her the truck keys. She was nervous as she tried to remember the sequence her grandfather had shown her the previous day. "Push down on the clutch, insert the small key, teeth up, turn back this way. Move the chrome lever to the left, pull the choke knob, push the small button on the left side of the dashboard," she mumbled to herself. The engine hummed. She pushed the choke knob in. She moved the stick shift over to the far left and up to put it into reverse, the top left *R* position of the H pattern shown on the knob. The transmission growled. She accelerated slowly and let out the clutch. The truck backed into the street and she stretched her neck to make sure there was no traffic. She turned the wheel sharply to the right, then shifted into first gear, the 1 at the bottom left of the H. Turning the corner, she accelerated and shifted to second gear, the 2 in the upper right, then to third at the bottom right of the

H pattern, the 3. They rolled east on 6th Avenue, once called Madrid Avenue. She turned right at the 1912 DeSoto Rural Graded School, now the maritime museum, onto 119th Street West and drove south to the shore of Palma Sola Bay. As they approached the Moondown tied to the pilings, a tall, angular man came out of the cabin. He was wearing a tee shirt and a pair of cutoff shorts, ragged above his knobby knees. A length of rope held his shorts up and secured a fishing knife in a leather scabbard. His bony arms were covered with thick, red hair. He was bare-footed.

"Hoyt, Cap'n. Got company, I see."

"Hands, this is Arianna just arrived from San Diego. She is Nathan's cousin."

"Nice to meet you, Arianna. I sure miss ole Nathan. I probably wouldn't be here today if it wasn't for him patching me up." He showed her the scars on his left arm. "Got a bigger scar on my chest, but I ain't gonna lift my tee shirt and show it to you. It's pretty gruesome."

"Musta hurt!" she grimaced.

"Sure did. Thought I was gonna die, but in the end it turned out alright. I'm still here, catching crabs, enjoying being out on the water, having fun."

Arianna looked up and saw Bubba One standing on the dock next to a very large boat with a big net and huge plastic foam floats piled high on the stern. She left B.D. and Hands standing there, both bewildered, as she rushed over to the teen-age boy and got right up in his face. "So, you're gonna give me a fat lip and a bloody nose, huh? I should wipe the yellow snot off my ugly face, huh? Let's see how brave you are with grown men around, Mr. Mighty Mouth!"

"Who are *y-you*?" the boy stammered.

"I'm that pimple-faced, snaggle-toothed, goober-lipped, stringy-haired, cross-eyed hyena. I'm that carpet-bagging, scalawag, old man Bradford's snooty, uppity grandkid from San Diego. That's who I am, and I'm gonna wash your mouth out with soap!"

"I never saw you in my life!" he screamed.

"Don't you lie to me, boy! You said all that awful stuff less than a half hour ago standing on the street at my grandpa's house, propped up against a palm tree like a pink flamingo."

"I've been right here on the Six Js since daybreak," he protested. "You must be talking about my twin brother."

Hands and B.D. moved in closer, not wanting to miss any of this fiery exchange, both snickering.

"It happens all the time," the boy explained. "My brother has a mean streak. He shoots his mouth off and then people get all over me for things he said and did. I'm innocent."

Hands walked up to them, forming his fingers into a T for timeout. Trying not to laugh, he explained to Arianna that the boys were identical twins and all their lives people mixed them up. "One's a smart mouth and the other's Mr. Nice Guy. You are talking to the nice guy, Bubba Two."

"Twins? Bubba Two? What's going on here?" She was stymied.

Bubba Two, frustrated, told her, "I'll never get used to it. People are always jumping my bones about stuff and I don't know anything. My brother is not a bad person, deep down, he just says whatever comes into his head. He can't filter his thoughts and he doesn't care what people think."

"What's with this Bubba One and Bubba Two?"

"Oh, he was born 14 minutes before I was, so our parents called us Brother One and Brother Two, which was soon shortened to Bubba One and Bubba Two. My twin somehow got the idea that he is my *older* brother and treats me like a little kid. Go figure. Tell me who you are."

Cooled down, she told him she was B.D.'s granddaughter visiting DeSoto during spring break, that she was finishing up the 10th grade in San Diego, and that her cousin Nathan had told her many good things about the village. She shook hands with Bubba Two.

Hands led Arianna back to the truck. "The two Bubbas look just alike, but they are very different. Everybody in the village knows how they are. Bubba One is the kind of guy who will take a stack of one dollar bills, wrap a hundred dollar bill on the outside, then fold the money, stick it in his pocket and take it out for show so people think he has a pocket full of hundred dollar bills. Bubba Two would take a stack of hundred dollar bills, wrap a one on the outside, then fold the money, stick it in his pocket, and keep it there."

B.D., Hands, and Arianna offloaded the traps from the back of the truck and stacked them neatly on the asphalt next to the Moondown. "We'll leave the traps here on land for a while. We won't be going crabbing for a week or so and I don't want the weight on the boat until we are ready to go out again, if the crabs ever show up."

CHAPTER 5
BAIT FISHING ON THE SIX JS

A large man with a deep voice came out of the wheelhouse of the Six Js, "Well, if we're going to catch any bait today, it's time to get started." Bubba Two quickly went back to work getting the boat ready. Hands also moved about the deck checking ropes and nets.

"Joe Mac," B.D. said to the captain, "this is my granddaughter, Arianna, visiting from San Diego. Arianna, this is Cap'n Joe Mac."

"Well, it's a pleasure young lady, welcome to DeSoto. How long are you going to be here?"

"Just a week," she told him.

"Want to go fishing?"

"Fishing? Me?"

"Yes, you. Your grandpa won't be stone crabbing till there's some crabs out there to be caught. Hands is working on the Six Js until crabs pick up again. We can use another pair of hands, that is, if you actually know how to use them." Joe Mac laughed gently.

Arianna looked at her grandfather with questioning eyes. He communicated back by shrugging his shoulders.

"I guess so. I know how to use my hands. What do I have to do?"

"Just watch the others. Hands will show you. Do what he says. I have oilers and boots on the boat that will fit you. Come aboard."

Cap'n Joe Mac led her to the wheelhouse and gave her a pair of orange oiler pants, Grundens, and white rubber boots. She slipped into the overalls and put on the boots. "All ready to go, I see," Cap'n Joe Mac approved. "You look like an experienced, sea-going sardine fisherman. Here, put this on." He handed her a ball cap with the embroidered logo of the Six Js and the word *crew* on the front.

"What does the name of the boat, Six Js, come from," she asked Cap'n Joe Mac.

"Good question," he said, "and I have a good answer. My parents had six kids, Janie, Johnny, Judy, Joe, Jackie, and Joyce. That's six family names beginning with J, so my boat is named Six Js.

Arianna helped Hands and Bubba Two lift the hatches away from the fishhold. Hands moved a big flexible tube and aimed it into the large opening in the deck of the boat. A loud motor came on and crushed ice shot out of the tube. Hands worked like a firefighter gripping the ice-spewing tube as it pushed back at him from the force. The crushed ice built up quickly in the fish hold and cooled the thick insulation of the walls and floor below.

"What's that for?" Arianna asked Cap'n Joe Mac.

"That's to chill the fish down. We pump in sea water to make a slurry, then bail the Spanish sardines from the net into the fishhold. The fish are at Gulf water temperature, this time of year around 70-75 degrees. We need to drop the temperature of the catch well below 40. By the time we load up the boat, the fish will be nice and cold, firm and solid, hard, but you won't see much unmelted ice left. That's when we head back to the barn and dip the sardines up into the wash bin at the dock. By nightfall, they will be all be packed in boxes, frozen, and stored away on metal racks. From the freezer, they go to market for the sports fishermen who catch big game fish, marlin, sailfish, swordfish, and tarpon. They have plenty of money so we get top dollar."

The crew replaced the hatch covers over the fishhold and untied the boat to push away from the dock, Hands on the bow line and Bubba Two on the stern line. Hands gave the bow a hard shove from the piling to head the boat into the channel.

"Hey, wait for me!"

Bubba One came running down the dock gripping his orange Grundens oilers, white boots cradled in his arms. He jumped high off the dock and landed on the net at the stern. The

Six Js eased away from the dock and entered the channel.

"Why is everybody in such a hurry? We got all day," he griped.

"You know the rules, Bubba One." Hands glowered at him. "You ain't here when the boat leaves the dock, you ain't fishin'. You ain't fishin', you ain't makin' no money. Means a bigger share for the crew that's on time and doin' the work."

Bubba One saw Arianna. "Don't tell me we got ole snaggle tooth on board. She ain't worth a half-share, much less a whole share. She don't know how to crew. She oughta pay us to learn how to fish." He stretched out on the net, folded his arms under his head and stared defiantly at the sky.

The crew left him there by himself and went into the wheelhouse where Cap'n Joe Mac was idling at no wake through the channel in the Kitchen, the broad, shallow area south of DeSoto where for generations the settlers caught fish and gathered scallops, clams, and conchs to feed their families.

"Look around you, Arianna," Hands motioned. "For over a hundred years, people in the village have been coming here and gathering food right out of the water. That's why they call it the Kitchen. I remember when I was real small, too young to go out and fish with the grown-ups, Stella and Louise brought us little ones out here at low tide to gather scallops. We all had a small open box with a window pane sealed in. It floated and we could look down into it and see the bottom through the glass, real clear. We had a small wash tub tied to our waist and scooped up the scallops into a wire screen tacked to the end of an old broom handle. We soon learned to put the scoop behind the square end of the scallop, the hinge, because it would squirt water and fly off in the grass if it sensed you were there. You get real good at it after a while and not many got away. It took a long time to fill the wash tub floating behind you, but we did it. Then we'd go over to Louise's back yard, all red and burned from the hot sun, and shuck the shells into the evening. They brought out the lanterns if it got too dark. I tell you, it was a problem when the mosquitoes and sand gnats came out. We called the tiny bugs sand gnats or *no-see-ums*, cause they were so little you couldn't see them. Then the moths would come to the lanterns. It was shuck, slap, shuck, rub, shuck, smack. It was also shuck, eat, shuck, eat and that's what made it good. We got to eat those sweet little scallops, raw, right out of the shell. Had to be real cool, though, or Stella would get on us. I think the best part, though, was just being there, knowing what you were doing was important, feeding the family, knowing you belonged, knowing you were loved, and loving those around you."

Hands was quiet in thought.

"Do people still gather scallops around here?" Arianna asked.

"Not so much," Hans told her. "The scallops got thinned out over the years. We might have taken them out of the water faster than they could fill back in. I read in the paper about storm water runoff filled with fertilizer, herbicides, and insecticides. We had a problem some years back with partially treated sewer water being released into the bay. I know the colleges are helping to bring the scallops back. The marine biologists take annual counts now and everybody is working together to bring the scallops back."

Bubba Two pointed out several small sheds out over the water in the Kitchen. "Those are called fish camps. Different fishermen built these and kept fishing gear in them. You can only reach them by water. Before the net ban, boat owners stored nets, rope, leads, corks, webbing, twine, mending needles, all kinds of gear. There is not much call for that now after the net ban, but a few camps survived. There used to be net spreads all over the water along the shore. It was easy to walk the narrow planks at the spreads and look for fish to gig."

"Gig?" Arianna asked.

"Well, yeah. People had these long poles with a sharp, three-prong, barbed metal end. The other end had a rope tied to it. If you wanted to gig a fish, you held the end of the coiled rope with one hand and with the other hand you aimed at the fish and let it fly. It really worked. It was a great way to get snook."

"Snook?"

Hands was listening carefully and had a wide grin as Bubba Two told her about village life.

"Well, yeah. Snook is a local fish, very strong and quick. They are the best for eating, firm flesh, white, not fishy. They like to swim near the surface, so they are easy to see. They are gray with a dark stripe the full length of the body on both sides. We sometimes call them stripers. Nowadays, there are a lot of complicated rules and regulations about catching snook, but they taste just as good now as they did back in the old days."

The Six Js passed Price's Key on the starboard side of the vessel and entered Anna Maria Sound, turning north into the Intracoastal Waterway, the ICW, and going under the Manatee Avenue Bridge. As the boat followed the channel up toward Gilligan's Island, it turned westerly. Seagulls followed the boat, sensing the odor of the sardines from the net on the stern. Bubba One lolled on the net and paid no attention to them. Arianna was absorbed by the birds looping and swerving behind the boat.

"Check this out!" Cap'n Joe Mac said to the crew in the wheelhouse. He pointed to the bow.

Arianna stood up and looked through the plexiglass windshield. Several fish were swimming alongside, some very large, rolling up through the sharp wake and diving again out of sight.

"Porpoises." Bubba Two said.

"They like to swim along with boats and roll in the wake." Hands added.

Arianna went out on the bow and stretched flat, holding her hand over the side. She could not reach the big fish, but got a close-up view of the porpoises and recognized the family grouping with large ones, several smaller adults, and a number of little ones. She heard the fish blow air and saw how they breathed through an opening at the top of the head when they rose out of the water and rolled in the rushing wake.

"They say they are as smart as we are," Bubba Two told her, sitting cross-legged on the bow. "I've heard stories about porpoises helping people get back to shore when they have gotten too far out in the water. They hang around our boat because they like sardines, too. They know it is a sardine boat. They can be a real problem if they get inside the net with a bunch of fish we have enclosed. Hard to get a porpoise out. All they want to do is eat, eat, eat. If they get tangled in the webbing, they'll drown, can't get any fresh air."

"Drown?" Arianna looked at him, amazed. "Fish can drown?"

"Sure enough. These are air breathers. No gills. If they can't get to the surface to breathe, they will die, just like people. Scientifically, they are not fish, not even porpoises. They are actually dolphins, mammals, not fish. "

"They look just like fish to me," Arianna mumbled. "They swim."

The Six Js continued west-northwest across lower Tampa Bay. "What's that over there?" Arianna asked Bubba Two, pointing to an island off to the right.

"Egmont Key. We are in the natural channel just south of Egmont. Off to our left is Passage Key. You can only see it at low tide since it is just a series of sandbars now. I've seen vegetation growing out there. Storms come in and the sand builds up. Stuff grows. Then storms come in and wash it all away. The history books say this is the very channel that Hernando DeSoto used almost five hundred years ago to bring his ships into Tampa Bay."

Arianna looked around, struck by the reality that she saw the same thing DeSoto and his crew saw when they sailed here from Spain and Cuba. Nothing had changed - not the water, not the sky, not the land.

"What's all that stuff there in the water?"

"That's an old fort." Bubba Two told her. "It used to be part of Egmont, but the sand got eaten away by storms and now all that's left are these huge slabs of concrete. There are several forts out here. Some washed away, some are still on land. There's one at Fort DeSoto that still has the big guns in it."

"Why would anyone build forts out here with big guns?"

"I don't know the whole story," Bubba Two said, "but an American Navy ship, the USS Maine, blew up in Havana harbor in 1898. Back then, Cuba belonged to Spain. Nobody knows what really happened, not to this day, but everybody got all riled up. The United States blamed Cuba and Spain declared war. The War Department built these forts to protect the area from invasion by ships. That war, the Spanish-American War, was short. I read where it only lasted ten weeks, but the forts are here forever. One of these days, I will take you over to Fort DeSoto on Mullet Key and you can see what the forts looked like when they were first built."

"Fishfinder, Fishfinder, this is the Six Js approaching from Egmont, over." Hands, Bubba Two, and Arianna joined Cap'n Joe Mac in the wheelhouse as he established radio contact with the airplane flying just ahead.

"Six Js, this is Fishfinder. Ready to haul bait?"

"Ready, Fishfinder. What do you see out there?"

"Couple of really big schools, one straight ahead."

"Roger that," Cap'n Joe Mac said into the microphone. "I want to take a look before we strike. Need to make sure it is the right stuff. The fishhouse doesn't want any more thread herring, so I'll take a look first. We'll take them in if it's Spanish sardines."

The crew members looked out of the plexiglass windows in the wheelhouse. Hands pointed to a large dark area in the water ahead. "There they are," he announced. They stretched and craned to see.

At a slow idle, the Six Js entered the mass of fish. The captain put the boat in neutral and stepped out onto the bow. The crew followed. He looked over the side and examined the catch. He checked the direction and speed of the mass as it moved slowly through the water. "Looks like the right stuff."

Hands and Bubba Two shouted together, "It's the right stuff, Cap'n!"

The Six Js motored away from the mass and positioned itself ahead of the movement in order to run the net in front of the school to cut it off, then race quickly all the way around to entrap the mass of sardines in a great circle.

"Let 'er go," Cap'n Joe Mac yelled. Hands and Bubba Two ran back to the stern to begin setting the net overboard.

"Hey, wait for me!"

Bubba One, suddenly awake, pulled on his oilers and boots.

Cap'n Joe Mac steered the Six Js rapidly ahead of the massive school to cut off its forward movement. The purse seine tumbled off the stern, forming a wall from the lead line at the bottom to the cork line at the top. The captain swung to the right around the mass, coming quickly up behind, then around the other side, returning to the start end of the net. Hands and Bubba Two worked together to hoist the tom weight with the hydraulic winch and drop it over the side of the boat. It made a noisy splash when it hit the water. *Squooloosh*! The tom weight rope sang as it uncoiled out of the blue cut-off plastic barrel on the deck and spun through the closed pulley overhead at high speed as the 300 pound, dome-shaped block of lead descended furiously to the sandy Gulf bottom to anchor one end of the bait net. The crew quickly pulled the two ends of the net together to seal in the catch with a wall of impenetrable webbing, from the sea bottom to the surface.

Arianna stood on deck just outside the wheelhouse and watched. Cap'n Joe Mac stood in the doorway. "Fishing is dangerous work, especially what they are doing," he said to her. "That tom weight would drag you to the bottom in a matter of seconds if you got tangled up in the line as it went down. If it snagged your ankle before the line passed through the block, it would jerk you up to the pulley and likely take your foot off. Gotta watch what you are doing on a fishing boat. Easy to get hurt, bad hurt, real bad."

Arianna saw what the captain was talking about. The line passing through the block seemed to give off ripples of heat. She could hear the block scream from friction and stress.

Hands operated the hydraulic winch on deck to cinch in the purse line attached to the tom weight, which held the net in place and kept it from rising off the bottom. Cinching works like a drawstring. The purse line runs from the tom weight to the other end of the net, the full length, through a series of stainless steel rings attached to the lead line at the bottom with bridals. As the rope is hauled in, the bottom of the net cinches together and closes the lead line under the mass of fish, thus making a cup shape and cutting off any chance for the sardines to escape under the bottom of the net. The fish are trapped, impounded. They cannot escape through the wall of the net, they cannot escape by sounding under the net because of the puckered lead line, and they cannot escape over the floating cork line at the surface.

"Fishfinder, Fishfinder, we have them penned. It's the right stuff."

"Roger that, Six Js. I'm heading back to the Bradenton-Sarasota airport. Let me know when you are ready to settle up. I could use a big payday. Fishfinder clear."

The two Bubbas hauled one end of the net back into the Six Js using the overhead hydraulic power block. Hands cinched the lead line into an ever smaller circle. Bubba Two handled the cork line and made sure it stacked neatly on the stern deck so it would play out cleanly on the next set without tangling. Arianna neatly stacked the webbing. Bubba One handled the lead line and rings. The net in the water was pulled together and the circle was made smaller and smaller. The huge school of sardines was slowly gathered into a tight, roiling mass. The cork line was pulled up along the side of the boat and draped over the rail. The sardines were bunched together, hardened up in a small circle so they could be bailed aboard and dropped into the ice hold. Arianna was amazed at the huge amount of fish caught in the net. The crew collected at the rail and looked down at the day's catch crowded and squirming at the side of the Six Js.

"There's a porpoise down there," Bubba Two shouted and pointed at the churning sardines. "We need to let him out. He'll drown if he gets hung up in the webbing."

"What kind of wimp are you?" Bubba One screamed. "So, the dumb porpoise got in the net. So what. He'll croak just like all these sardines will. Who cares? Let the stupid porpoise die!"

"We have to let him out," Bubba Two insisted.

"You want to let him out? Let him out!" He shoved his twin brother overboard, into the thick mass of struggling, flopping sardines.

Hands grabbed Bubba One and threw him forcefully onto the net piled up on the stern, then climbed over the side. He reached Bubba Two's hand and pulled him back to the boat. The two crewmen clung to the webbing hanging from the rail. Hands yelled to Arianna, "Push that boom over here. That steel pipe with the pulley hanging down."

Arianna understood and quickly pushed the boom out over the catch. Steadied by Hands, Bubba Two grabbed the open pulley on the boom, hoisted himself, and balanced on top of the cork line. It sank below the water line. A few feet away, Hands also stepped down on the cork line with his feet. Sardines swam over the submerged cork line between them, soon followed by the big porpoise, seeing its own chance to escape over the cork line. The porpoise rose to the surface, blew air, inhaled, and swam away, chasing the sardines newly freed from the net. The crew stepped off the cork line and it resumed its sentry work in keeping the rest of the fish in the pen.

Hands and Bubba Two climbed back over the rail. They sat down, emptied sea water out of their boots, and put them back on again, wet and soggy.

"You two happy? Did you boy scouts do your good deed for the day?" Bubba One sassed. "We lost over a hundred dollars' worth of fish just to let that dumb porpoise out. Wish it had been a shark. You'd really be sorry."

"We got work to do! Bail the sardines in!" Cap'n Joe Mac commanded from the wheelhouse.

Bubba One, grumpy and surly, slotted the line of the big bailer into the pulley hanging from the end of the steel boom. Hands explained to Arianna how to push the boom and bailer out over the catch, then bring the load back, full of fish, and hold it steady over the ice hold where the catch would be released from the bailer and fall into the icy slurry. She pushed the boom out. Bubba One controlled the bailer and held the rope that cinched the bailer net shut. Bubba Two operated the hydraulic equipment to lower the bailer into the fish and then raise it back up to be swung over the ice hold. Bubba One aimed the front ring of the bailer down into the mass of sardines. He worked it around inside the mass of fish. Bubba Two tightened the line with the hydraulic winch. The bailer came up high, filled with fish. Arianna pushed the boom on its swivel over the ice hold. When Bubba One loosened the rope he held tight on the bailer shaft, the bailer net opened at the bottom and released the fish. The crew repeated this ritual over and over until all the sardines were in the ice. They brought the rest of the net on board, hauled the tom weight, and cleaned up the deck. The Six Js had a full boatload of Spanish sardines - 30,000 pounds - iced up and ready for market. Pulled well down into the water by the weight of the catch, the fishing boat slowly returned to the Gulf to Bay Seafood Company in the old village of DeSoto.

Arianna once again manned the boom as the crew worked in reverse from offshore to get the sardines off the boat and onto the dock. Bubba One pushed the end of the bailer down into the ice hold and filled it with fish. Bubba Two worked the equipment to raise the loaded bailer. Arianna pushed the boom over to the dock. Bubba One released the rope holding the bailer net together at the bottom and the fish fell onto a large hopper with a conveyor belt that transported the catch up to the top of a stainless steel tank for a final rinsing in fresh water. Heavy-gauge, orange plastic webbing covered the hopper and the conveyer to keep out the pelicans. It was impossible to shoo them away. Those ever-hungry birds were gathered in large numbers near the Six Js, hoping to get dinner from the catch. They scarfed up every sardine they could reach, snatching the ones that fell to the concrete floor at the instant they hit. Another conveyer belt brought the clean, ice-cold fish out of the fresh water and dropped them in piles onto a sorting table. The fishhouse crew packed the small Spanish sardines into plastic bags and placed them in boxes of 25 pounds each. The boxes were stacked onto steel racks and wheeled into the freezer with the fork lift. When the quota for 25 pound boxes was met, the shift was made to 5 pounds boxes. The work dropped to a very slow pace as the fish house employees worked as fast as they could to pack and weigh the small boxes. It was a time-consuming task to fill the small plastic bags by hand, weigh them to assure correct poundage, then place them in a small white cardboard box. It was full dark when the Six Js crew finally had all the fish off the boat, the decks scrubbed clean, and the equipment washed down and properly stored.

Bubba Two walked Arianna home from the dock. They stood together at the steps. "What my brother did today was wrong, wrong from the start when he showed up late again. If you are going to be a dependable crew member, you have to be there early to get the boat ready to fish. He was late, showing up at the last minute, so Hands and I had to do his job."

"Well," Arianna quickly jumped in, "being late was nothing compared to him pushing you off the boat and into the fish. What if that had been a shark down there and not a porpoise?"

"Yeah. Well, I guess I was lucky."

"Yeah, u-huh, *lucky*. Bubba One could have killed you."

"Don't be too hard on him. Down deep I think he's OK."

"We'll see," Arianna said. "We'll see."

"You have a boyfriend out in California?" Bubba Two asked.

"Not at the moment. Why are you asking?"

Turning red, he croaked, ""I'd like a date."

"I'll think about it." She bent forward, kissed him on the cheek, then hurried into the house.

CHAPTER 6
ARIANNA MEETS PAT

The light came bright into the bedroom, even though filtered by the three ancient mango trees in the side yard to the east of the house. Arianna forced herself awake, feeling the pull of the muscles in her arms, back and legs. "Sardine fishing is hard work!" she muttered to herself, pulling on cutoff shorts and the Skyway Jack's tee shirt, careful not to make any sudden moves to set off muscle cramps. She heard the antique wall clock sound seven times.

"Ugh. Seven in the morning! I could sleep all day." She followed the coffee smell into the kitchen, poured a cup, stirred in cream and sugar. She saw someone sitting on the steps outside the screen door.

"Hi, Arianna, I'm Pat. Cap'n Bradford told me you were here. Said you were out yesterday bait fishing for Spanish sardines on the Six Js. I'm a friend of Nathan's, your cousin. I made the coffee."

"Oh, Pat, I am really glad to see you. Nathan told me so much about you. He said you helped them on the Moondown when the engine overheated. Said you were a first-rate diesel mechanic, plus a lot more. I was going to find you this morning. Nathan said to say hello."

They sat together.

"How do you like bait fishing?" Pat asked her.

"Tough, hard work," she responded. "Dangerous, too. Handling that big net is the hardest part. Scooping the fish into the bait hold is tough, too, even with the hydraulic gear. Clearing the catch at the fishhouse is the pits. It takes forever to get the sardines off the boat, washed through the freshwater tank, then sorted into boxes for freezing. We did fine on the twenty-five pound cartons, but when it came to filling the little five pound boxes, it took forever, even with lots of people just flying into the fish and packing them as fast as possible. You ever catch Spanish sardines?"

"Oh, yes," Pat said. "I've been out on the Six Js with Cap'n Joe Mac a bunch of times. It is always hard work, but one thing is certain, we always load the boat with fish. Not like that with crabs. Your grandpa had to take his traps in and put them on the hill. The octopus moved in and ate up the stone crabs. It wasn't worth the fuel, bait, and time, plus the wear and tear on the equipment to clear and re-bait the traps. A good storm might mix things up a little and get the crabs to crawl, but we'll just have to wait until the crabs recover. Maybe over the summer during closed season, more crabs will migrate in and we can do better next fall in the new season. I just don't see how anyone can make a living out of stone crabs, but every crabber keeps hoping that next year will be better."

"Put the traps on the hill? There are no hills around here."

"Oh," Pat laughed, "that's what crabbers say when they take their traps out of the water and store them on land. 'Put the traps on the hill,' they say, even when there is not a hill in sight. It's a saying and everybody around here knows what it means. It's like when they say they are heading the boat back to the barn. They mean back to the dock. Even while they stack the traps on the hill, they all talk about how next year is going to be better. I heard one old crabber, O'Leary, tell your grandpa, 'As long as I can keep on borrowing money from the fishhouse, I'm gonna keep on stone crabbing.'

"Let's take a walk." Pat tucked in her t-shirt with silhouettes of 3 mullet and the words, *Proud to Be a DeSoto Kid*. The two young women stopped at the old Alvah Taylor house across the street. "This was one of the few houses in DeSoto that was built by a real architect from a formal design. Most of the houses in DeSoto started out as small, one-room, frame buildings. People cooked, ate, slept, washed and made do in just one single room. As they caught fish and saved money, they would get lumber and add a room, build a porch, then screen the porch to use as a sleeping room during the hot summer months. It was pay as you go. These tack-ons ended up with some strange roof designs. Look at this place. It's the old Joe Bradford house. The original one-room got added to on all four sides, with a kitchen and bathroom in back, an entry porch in front out of the weather, and bedrooms on the two sides."

"Oh," Pat said, "Grandpa told me about this place. Is this the one where the stop netters dynamited the sleeping porch?"

"Yep, this is the place." Pat led Arianna to the front and knocked. Linda came to the door and recognized Pat. "Come in, come in," she repeated.

"Linda, this is Arianna. She's B.D. Bradford's granddaughter from San Diego. She's Nathan's cousin. You remember him when he was here last Thanksgiving. Pat heard all about the big fight between the stop netters and the traditional fishermen, how the stop netters dynamited Joe's house to shut him up, teach him a lesson. Joe was trying hard to get stop-netting outlawed by the state and he let everybody know how he felt. Show Arianna where it happened."

"It was a real fight," Linda said. "The stop netters strung long nets across bayous and inlets, trapping every swimming thing. They hauled nets with powerful motors, they called them donkeys, and dragged the fish over to big scows. The whole catch was scooped up, food fish, trash fish, crabs, turtle grass, whatever was in the net. There could be 30,000 to 40,000 pounds of squirming, flopping mess. The catch would be brought to the fishhouse and sorted out, setting the food fish aside for washing, weighing, and icing. The rest got thrown back into the scows and shoveled overboard behind one of the mangrove keys. It was a very wasteful way to fish and the State of Florida eventually banned stop netting."

Linda led them into the house and to the sleeping porch on the north side. "See, the doorway was splintered. This is the original door jamb and you can see where long strips were blown away, then just painted over. Same thing over here at the window. They meant to kill him! This was serious business and the stop netters were not going to allow anyone to force them to quit. They made real money out of stop netting.

If Joe had not gone to the outhouse in the wee hours, he would have been blown to smithereens." Arianna shuddered.

Walking south, Pat showed Arianna the old Church of the Rock. "That was a church for a long time," she told Arianna. "It was a fundamental, 'if the Bible says it, I believe it' kind of church. Most of the preachers were self-educated. The parsonage was right next door and a few preachers managed to eke out an existence from parishioners who did not have much to share. Eventually, the congregation evaporated and the church and parsonage were bought by the DeSoto Village Historical Society. It is now used for community meetings and has a new name, Bradford Hall, in honor of one of the pioneer families."

Arianna was impressed that the village elders honored the contributions made by the original pioneer families that settled the tiny fishing hamlet in the 1880s, coming here from the Chesapeake Bay. She was gaining an appreciation for the accomplishments of her forebears, knowing that she was a sixth generation descendent of Nettie Bradford.

"This next house is one of the oldest in the village. It was built out along the shore around the turn of the century, then moved here by the Kringle family in 1915. There is a famous artist living there now named Linda Molto. She does really nice work with waterfront settings, lots of boats, tropical birds and flowers. That's her studio." Pat pointed to a small building near the back of the lot. "As time goes by, more and more artists and writers will settle here in DeSoto to live and work."

"And that is G.P. Brevis Seafood," Pat pointed to a large complex of buildings along the shore. "G.P. started the fishhouse many years ago and his descendants carried it on. Most of them are now gone, so his great great granddaughter runs the place. Her name is Karenia Brevis."

"Oh," Arianna said, "Nathan told me about her. Sued all the fishermen to collect on the company store accounts. She paid process servers to hand them official papers. The fishermen were forced to hire lawyers to defend themselves in state court. Times must have gotten hard for her to sue like that for money."

"Yep, times had to be hard," Pat smirked. "Not only did she sue the fishermen, she recorded liens against their homes, clouding their title. If and when they sell the property, the courts will collect for her and give her the money. Even so, she still had enough cash on hand to buy the Astra Fish Company next door and turn it into a restaurant. Karenia threw away four generations of square dealing by the Brevis family. None of the locals will bring their fish to Brevis anymore. Greed is not good."

"Want to have lunch at Astra Fish Company?" Arianna asked impishly.

"No way. I dare not set foot on any Brevis property. My grandpa would never speak to me again if I did. He is very bitter about the fishhouse suing him and the other fishermen. She sued your grandpa, too. He's just as mad as my grandpa. They teamed up, got a lawyer, and won big time in court. They have an official court order that says they do not owe Karenia Brevis one red cent.

"Let's walk down to the Kitchen. We can have lunch there."

CHAPTER 7
VILLAGE TOUR

The young women walked down the central street of the village, once called Madrid Avenue, and turned right at the DeSoto Rural Graded School, walking on down to the Kitchen, an open-air, dockside restaurant. Over grouper sandwiches, Arianna asked, "What was here before the settlers came down from the Chesapeake Bay?"

"Not much," Pat said, chewing, "There were Spanish fish camps all up and down the southwest coast of Florida. The fishermen sailed up from Havana and made camps to catch and process fish for shipment back to Cuba, and then on back to Spain. They called the fish camps *ranchos*. Mother ships came to rotate fresh crews and to bring supplies: hooks, twine, net webbing, corks, lead weights, rope, salt, stuff like that, barrels to store fish in, rice, flour, lard, cooking oil, pots and pans, buckets, whatever was needed. The mother ships would take back the accumulated catch: salted, smoked, sun-dried, pickled and brined, all stored away in barrels, ready to eat."

"Just mullet?" Arianna asked.

"Probably everything," Pat said. "If they could catch it and preserve it, they probably did just that. I'm sure there were seasonal efforts like mullet and mullet roe in the late fall. I know local grouper fishermen have hauled large anchors up from the Gulf that date back to the early 1800s, probably made in a foundry in Havana, possibly in a blacksmith shop at a shipyard on the southern coast of Spain. There's one of those anchors in your grandpa's back yard. So it is pretty certain there were boats offshore in the Gulf catching grouper with hand lines."

Pat held her fish sandwich out, "Just the same grouper as we are eating."

"What about stone crabs?" Arianna asked.

"Who knows? Maybe they figured out a way to preserve the claw meat. It would be quite a delicacy. I imagine the people in the fish camps must have known about stone crabs and harvested them for their own use, at least. I know I would. They are gooood! Blue crabs, too! And, surely, they ate oysters, scallops, clams, and conchs."

"What was here before the Cuban fish camps, the ranchos?" Arianna followed up her inquiry.

"Indians. Native Americans. Aborigines. We read a lot about Indians in Florida, Seminoles and Miccosukee, but when Ponce de Leon explored in 1513 and then DeSoto landed in 1539, near here, the Indians were different. There were quite a few villages back then with many indigenous people. Locally, there was the Tanpa tribe down near Charlotte Harbor. That's where Tampa got its name, even though the Spanish navigators confused the 28 line with the 27 line and ended up further north in what they named, in error, Tampa Bay."

"What's the 27 line, the 28 line?"

"Oh," Pat said. "Those are lines of latitude. The 27 line is 27 degrees north of the equator. It is where Charlotte Harbor and Ft. Myers are located. The 28 line is 28 degrees above the equator. That is where Tampa Bay and Tampa are located.

"Check these Indian tribal names: Mayaimi, Ocale, Alachua, Appalachee. They are all places in Florida today. Where we are sitting now, right this minute, was the home of the Colusa tribe, the ones the Spanish conquistadores called the *fierce people.* They lived all over the wetlands and coastal rivers in southwest Florida. The name of the Colusahatchee River came from that tribe."

"Are these tribes still around?"

"Nope. The Europeans brought in smallpox and measles. The tribes had no resistance to those foreign plagues. What the diseases didn't kill, warfare with the invaders did. By 1800, all the tribes that were here when the Spanish came were gone, extinct. A few remnants joined other tribes further north. That's when the Seminoles and Miccosukee, part of the Creek Nation, farther north moved into Florida and settled."

"How can you be so sure?"

"Spanish ships' logs. Memoirs of explorers. History books. Indian mounds."

"What's that?"

"Piles of shell."

"I don't understand." Arianna told her.

"The people living here when the Europeans made contact ate every kind of shellfish, you know, oysters, clams, scallops, whelk, conch, plus fish and crabs of every kind. They could pretty much wade out in the water and gather their food. We know they used nets because we have found remnants with large, heavy shells used to hold down the bottom line and dried empty gourds to float the top line of the net. They wove palm fibers into rope and cord and knotted webbing for nets. When they finished a meal, they ended up with lots of shells and fish bones. These were hauled off and discarded. Over hundreds of years, even thousands of years, the shells piled up. They also used the mounds to throw stuff away, like broken pottery, old shell and gourd dippers, ornaments, tools, all kinds of unwanted junk, arrow heads and spear heads, many with the tips broken off. Archeologists call the piles *middens*. They have found bones from white-tail deer and small animals, fish heads, turtle shells. Some of the mounds are up like 20 or 30 feet high and as long as a football field. The mounds are a collection of the debris of daily life."

"Are there any mounds around here?" Arianna asked, really interested.

"Yes, right here in DeSoto. One of the old timers in the village used to dig in the local mounds when he was a boy years and years ago. He has a collection of artifacts like pieces of pottery, shells with holes drilled in them to be used for decoration and jewelry, plus many arrow heads and spear points made out of chert and flint. The local tribes must have traded with other Indians who travelled on foot bartering flint. There's certainly no flint around here. The old timer's name is Lyman Roughy. It would be great while you are here if we could visit with him and see all his stuff."

"That would be neat. I would like that." Arianna responded. "Where are the mounds Lyman dug in?"

"Gone," Pat said. "It's like Mr. Peabody's coal train came in and hauled them away."

"Gone?"

"Yep. When roads were first built in this area, the shell was hauled away on big dump trucks and used as the bed for new roads. It happened all over Florida. Lyman told me once that he could take me right where there are still a few shells, but the area is all houses now and on private land. Would you like to see Indian mounds?"

"Yes, yes," Arianna said excitedly.

"All right. Let's find your grandpa. If he will let us use the old Ford truck, we'll drive over to Emerson Point and I will show you how life was in Florida quite a few thousand years ago. Do you have a driver's license?"

"Sure do!"

CHAPTER 8
THE INDIAN MOUNDS AT EMERSON POINT

"Pull in here to the left," Pat told Arianna as they drove to the end of Emerson Point. They parked the 1939 Ford truck, walked along the shore line and looked out over the water where the tidal Manatee River joined Tampa Bay.

"This hasn't changed much in the past three or four thousand years," Pat said. "What you see now is what the Colusa Indians saw, exactly what DeSoto and his crew saw. I read where archeologists found evidence of human activity in Florida as long as 12-14 thousand YBP, Years Before Present. The most recent ice age stopped its advance southward some 14,000 years ago. Hunters worked east to west back then stalking mastodons and wooly mammoths with spears. There were giant sloths and saber-toothed tigers. These are the same animals they dug out of the LaBrea Tar Pits in Los Angeles. Our teachers in school called the big animals *megafauna.* The climate was cooler and drier back then. We found Florida artifacts that connect to the Clovis culture in what is now New Mexico, especially flint arrow heads and spear points that have the distinct Clovis design. What I find interesting is that a bison skull was recovered from the gravel bottom of a slow-moving river. It had a flint spear point imbedded in the bone."

"You mean there were people here all that time ago?"

"Oh, yes," Pat said. "I don't know if they were always the same people during all that time. As the mile-thick ice sheet melted, sea level rose and flooded large areas. Florida's west coast used to go out about 100 miles more than what we see now. They say that there are natural freshwater wells out in the Gulf that once formed the center of life for villages. Fishermen today look for those upwellings of fresh water because, for some reason, large numbers of fish hang out near them. If we could explore down there we might find all kinds of tools, pottery, and stuff where the Indians lived."

"That's exciting! I think it would be fun to be an archeologist and dig up stuff from the past, especially under water."

"Well, there's plenty to dig up right around here. We have Weedon Island and the Safety Harbor settlements just north of here that archeologists will examine for many years to come. The science books tell us that sea level stabilized about three thousand years ago, so the outline of Florida has been steady for quite a while. We have evidence locally of settlements dating back 4,500 years."

"Where are the Indian mounds?"

"Turn around." Pat said.

Arianna turned around and saw a long hill at the water's edge. "That's big!"

"Yep, must be twenty feet high and at least two hundred feet long. Just imagine how many oysters, scallops, clams, conchs, and fish bones it took to make that trash pile."

"And how many years it took! C'mon, let's go!" She grabbed Pat's hand and the girls raced up to the top of the mound.

"This is a great view from up here. I can see a lot more. What's that out there?" Arianna pointed over the water to the west.

"Anna Maria Island, the northern end, Bean's Point, then further out to the right is Egmont Key. What you see right now is the same as what the Indians saw hundreds, thousands of years ago. That's what DeSoto saw, too, from over there," Pat pointed across the water, "from the other side of the Manatee River." She pointed out a low, tan-colored building on the far bank. "That's the place where DeSoto is said to have landed in 1539. You can see the flag at the entrance to the park if you look carefully at the top of the trees over there."

Pat pointed toward the north. "There's the Sunshine Skyway. Look over at Egmont. If you focus on the end to the right, there should be a flash from the lighthouse beacon."

"Saw it! There it is." They stood in awe of the realization that the land and water around them was unchanged from the earliest times of human habitation and that Hernando DeSoto's eyes had viewed the same panorama.

"Why do they call this the Manatee River?" Arianna asked.

"Oh, that's easy. The river is named after the manatee, a huge, blubbery mammal. They are called sea cows. They live in warm climates at the mouth of tidal rivers like this one, so they can go from fresh water to salt water and back."

"Ever see one?"

"Oh, yes, all the time. I saw a mother and calf not long ago, right in the village. The mom was nearly 10 feet long and the baby was at least 6 feet. Grown manatees get up over 1,200 pounds. You can see one anytime you want."

"Just standing up here on the Indian mound?"

"Well, why not? You can see clear across the river from up here. What I meant was that we can visit a real live manatee at the South Florida Museum. He's called Snooty and he has a deluxe aquarium to live in. They say he is the world's oldest living manatee at 64. We can go visit him anytime you like."

"That would be great," Arianna said. She looked around from high above the water. "It must have been a lot of work to drag the shells up here. And smelly, too. And flies! Ick! How did they stand the stench and the bugs?"

"My theory," Pat answered, "is that the kids had to drag the garbage up here in skin sacks and dump it. If I were doing it, I would want some help, so maybe two or three kids together might have worked garbage detail. One thing they had to do was keep all the shells in the same limited area, out of the way and not underfoot."

"Did people make camp right here near the mound?" Arianna asked.

"I doubt it. These were intelligent people and knew better than to camp right next to the dump, smell the shells and endure the flies. They had enough trouble with mosquitos, fleas, gnats, ticks, and other biting insects."

"Can we dig here?"

"No can do. Florida has all kinds of laws against taking artifacts, even on private land. In the public parks, the rangers are always on the lookout." Pat pointed to a warning sign that announced a fine of $5,000 and 5 years in jail for disturbing the area. There were many other signs telling people what they could not do. There were no signs or displays telling about the shell mound and its history.

This time Pat drove the truck back along 17th Street West and stopped at the Portavan Temple Mound.

"Temple Mound?" Arianna looked at Pat.

"Some historians surmise that the mounds were used for religious purposes and thus were called temple mounds. I don't think there was anything around here as complex as the Aztecs in Mexico, where there were human sacrifices at the top of their stone pyramids and other gory stuff."

"What about dead people? Did they bury the dead in the mounds?"

"I don't think it was a local custom. Researchers have found human remains in mounds. One book I read talked about how remains were left outside at the top of mounds for vultures and critters and bugs to work over and leave just the bones, picked clean. These were collected, bagged, and retained by the family to honor the dead. But I don't know if everybody did that or just some. When you stand way up on top of a mound and look around, the place takes on special meaning and I can understand how they might be seen as unique places to think and contemplate."

Pat pulled the truck into a tree-shaded parking area just off the road. "You'll like this," she told Arianna. They hiked in under great oaks and gumbo limbo trees, then up a steep wooden ramp. "Lemons," Arianna observed, as they ascended the ramp. She pointed to the left where the branches of a citrus tree were filled with yellow fruit.

"That may be the last lemon tree left," Pat told her. "Right after the Civil War, settlers started coming into Florida. The Griffiths homesteaded this site in 1866. He was a major in the Confederate Army. They grew oranges and lemons. They brought in and planted a lot of banana trees, too, but I've never seen any around here. They raised vegetables as well."

"How do you know all that?"

"I've been here before, many times, and read the signs over and over," Pat replied. "It is one my favorite things to do."

At the top of the ramp, Pat pointed to the Manatee River several hundred feet away. "Just like the Indians, the pioneers travelled by water. Major Griffith had a dock down there and boated up river to the little town of Manatee to sell his harvest and to buy supplies. There was a house right here with a long open porch facing the river. It's all grown over now with brush and vines. You can see the chimney," she said, pointing to several large pieces of masonry lying on the ground at the top of the ramp. "See those big slabs? That is called tabby. The builders mixed crushed shell, sand, and lime made from burning oyster shells in an open fire. They made thick mortar out of the mixture, then poured it on site into forms for support foundations and walls. You can see where they used brick for the actual fire place, then poured the tabby to form the hearth and chimney. Look here. You can see shells as part of the mortar mix." Pat pointed to bits of shell in the chimney debris. "Behind you are the remains of the old cistern. They used wooden and metal gutters and downspouts to direct all the rainwater into the cistern so they had a reliable fresh water supply."

"Where's the Indian mound you told me about?"

"You're standing on it," Pat replied. "Remember the ramp we had to climb back there? This hill is man-made."

"But it is all grown over. The mound we just visited was clear. There were no trees or bushes, just some grass here and there and weeds."

"Well, over time stuff grew here and never got cleared out. The other site was spruced up and set back to its original appearance. Almost any little hill you find around here could be a shell midden, trees or no trees."

Arianna was completely taken by the old home site. She read the displays that told interesting details about the history of the old homestead.

There was even a photograph of the small house built on top of the mound with an open porch running along the front, facing the river. The house was built high up to take advantage of the cool Gulf breezes, well above any flood line, and had a picture-perfect view of the Manatee River to the south. There was also a photograph of the large flat area below the mound. A lane went down to the river framed by two rows of royal palm trees. She was astounded to look down and see that same lane below her. Many of the royal palms were gone, but there were still a few and it was easy to see how pleasant and orderly the homestead was when the pioneers settled there.

They followed the plank walkway at the top of the mound and stood in front of a framed historical marker. It told the story of Peter and Golden Marine who settled on the site in 1910 and how, in 1922, they died together in a tragic accident. She tried to save Peter floundering in the river and they both drowned.

At the bottom of the wooden ramp, they wandered along the royal palm lane down to the

Manatee River. Standing on the modern dock out in the water, the girls were deeply moved, looking at the wide, peaceful river and thinking about the couple that drowned just offshore from where they stood.

"Do you suppose they were in some kind of boat, or did they just wade out into the river?" Arianna asked.

"Maybe they had one of those dugout canoes. When Nathan was here, we saw one over at DeSoto Landing. The Indians would take a pine log and shape the outside into a boat, then chip at the wood to hollow out a canoe. They built small fires along the trunk where they wanted to remove the wood, let the flame die down, then scraped out the charcoal left behind. Must have taken forever. They used clam shells and stones for scrapers. Pine is hard and they had no real tools. They liked pine, though, because it was filled with sap, making it resistant to bugs and to rot. It lasted a long time."

"It is really sad," Arianna whispered. "They worked so hard to make a good life here, free and independent, but it just got the best of them.

We have so much and they had so little, truly, almost nothing. We take a hot shower whenever we want and don't even think about it, we eat food of every kind, wear clean clothes, sleep in warm beds with cotton sheets. If they got sick, they were lucky if they did not just die right then and there. We can buy any kind of fish at any supermarket. If they wanted fish, they had to catch it. If they wanted fruits and berries, they had to gather them."

"Yes," Pat agreed. It was a tough life back then, simpler, but a lot more work and a lot less play."

Pat drove the truck back to DeSoto and as they passed the post office, Pat saw Lyman Roughy coming out the door. She pulled the truck up to him, rolled down the window, and shouted, "Hey, Lyman."

"Hey, sugar booger, how you doing? How's your old grandpa Howard?"

"I'm fine, he's fine. This is Arianna, Cap'n B.D.'s granddaughter. She's visiting from San Diego. We want to ask you a favor."

"And what might that favor be?"

"We want to see where the old shell mounds were here in DeSoto."

"Sure, baby doll, when you want to do that?"

"How about now?" Pat grinned. "Hop in the truck."

Arianna slid over and Lyman got in. "Drive over to the north side of Manatee Avenue from 127th Street, past my house," he instructed.

The area was completely built out with expensive houses and condos crowded together. Lyman's place was the oldest one on the north side of the village. He built it himself before the days of home air conditioning and filled the walls with windows to create cross ventilation to cool the house.

"Right there." He pointed to a small mound overgrown with hibiscus. "That's all that's left. I come here as a boy and dug all the time, but when they built the paved road, the dump trucks hauled the shell away to use as a foundation. It's a shame."

"You still have your collection of arrow heads and stuff?"

Pat asked.

"Sure do. Wanna see it?"

The girls lit up. "Can't wait," Arianna shouted.

Pat pulled the truck into Lyman's driveway under the live oak trees.

Lyman opened an Army foot locker and lifted out the tray. "Here they are," he announced.

Eyes were bright and focused as they scanned the collection of ancient artifacts. "Can we touch them?" Arianna asked.

"Sure."

They sorted through the collection. "These must be really old." Pat said.

"They are that," Lyman answered, "could be thousands of years old." He lifted two matching arrow heads from the tray. "Be right back."

The girls looked at the spear heads in the bottom of the foot locker, some whole, many broken off. They picked up shattered pieces of clay pottery and various shells with holes drilled in them for use as decoration, or, for the larger, heavier pieces, as weight for the nets. When Lyman returned, he carefully hung an arrow head tied with a leather thong around Pat's neck and another arrow point over Arianna's head. "I know you will like these," he smiled.

"I'll never take it off," Arianna squealed, kissing the arrow head. "Thank you, Lyman, thank you." She smacked him on the cheek. "Is this legal?"

"Sure is, honey. I found all this stuff before there was a law against collecting it. I'm so old I'm grandfathered in, heh, heh."

Pat hugged him in gratitude. Lyman smiled.

CHAPTER 9
DUGOUT CANOE

Arianna pulled the covers up higher, dimly aware of the old wall clock in the living room as it ticked off the minutes and hours. She was transported back to an earlier time.

She looked up from the pump as she worked the handle and filled the bucket. He was coming back from the river carrying a gig over his shoulder and a fresh-caught fish with a narrow dark stripe the length of its body. He carried a wet sack. She met him at the back porch as he came up the slope. "Oh, dinner. That is a very nice fish you have, sir. Looks mighty tasty." She gave him a swift peck on the cheek.

"*This, my dear, is one of the tastiest fish ever known, a snook, all solid white meat. I dressed it on the canoe. All it needs is a little salt, plus a touch of pepper. If you will do the honors of seasoning, I will get the fire going to turn this into our dinner this evening.*"

He started with leaves and Spanish moss to start the fire, then added small twigs, then larger pieces until the fire was ready for the dry, thick branches of button wood from inland mangrove. "Ah," he said to himself, " this is the wood that gives food a special fragrance and taste." She laid the fish, ready to cook on palmetto fronds next to the stone cooking circle. He poked at the coals burning red and spread them around. He set the metal grill over the coals and let it get hot. He stretched the fish flat with the skin down, exposing the two filets. She gathered tomatoes, green onions, and tender lettuce from the small, flat garden terraced into the side of the mound and dressed with black soil.

She picked a yellow lemon and cut it into wedges for the fish.

They ate at the table on the porch and looked out to the river, pleased at the end of another day of free, independent living. He removed the oysters from the wet sack and set them out on a palmetto frond. He shucked one for her. She took it off the shell. He ate one, then they took turns one after the other until all that was left was a pile of empty oyster shells. She squeezed lemon juice on her fish and ate, marveling at the freshness and good taste of the snook he brought to the table and cooked on the open fire. He dressed his salad with the glass olive oil and vinegar containers and marveled at the freshness and good taste of the salad she gathered in the garden.

They took their bedding outside and stretched side-by-side as night came, looking into the clear, star-filled sky. "Look," she whispered, "a shooting star." They snuggled closer as the night air cooled.

Arianna pulled the sheet up and wiggled under the comforter to stay warm. She gripped the arrow head tight as she dropped back into deep sleep.

"Why don't you come with me today," he said as the sky lightened. "You like being out on the water. There's plenty of room in the dugout canoe."

She was excited about going out onto the river with him. They had worked months on making the dugout, pulling the old pine log out of the river, shaping it into the form of a canoe, burning and chipping out the inside, just like the Indians did centuries before. He thought it was a manatee when he first saw it floating offshore, but when he realized it was a pine log, he waded out, then swam out to bring it to shore. They let it dry and mounted it on sable palm logs to work the hard, difficult wood. He tapered the two ends and gave the log its basic canoe shape. They built fires along the length to hollow it out for seating. They were very careful to tend the fires and move them around to char the wood and make it easier to scrape and chisel out. The canoe became very important for their life on the river. It allowed them to leave the shore and made it easier to catch fish to eat. The dugout canoe gave them a sense of connection to the past.

She sat in the back and slowly paddled the heavy craft. He faced the front on his knees, looking for a fish to gig. He stood up to get a better view. He motioned to her to paddle to the left. He pulled the gig back and aimed, holding the coiled rope in the other hand. She felt the canoe move sharply as he lost his balance and fell forward. She watched his head strike the hard wooden bow as he fell into the river. She saw blood on the surface. He sank slowly. She threw herself into the water and hugged her arms tight around his chest, pulling and tugging to bring him to the surface. She kicked her feet back and forth. She could swim, she could bring him back up. They sank together. She would not let him go, fading without air, dizzy. She felt the bottom and got her legs under him. Gripping his chest tight, she pushed hard with both legs against the sandy bottom to bring them to the surface and fresh air.   .   .

Arianna woke, frightened, gasping for breath, pushing hard against the mattress with her feet, gripping tight the arrow head on the leather thong around her neck.

CHAPTER 10
JET SKIS

Arianna heard the screen door rattle back and forth against the door jamb and a voice yelled, "Anybody home?" She saw one of the Bubbas holding his hands together over his eyes, shielding them, and looking into the house.

"I just hope you're Bubba Two," she said bluntly through the screen door.

"That I am," he grinned back at her. She stepped out onto the cement steps and motioned for him to sit down. She took the spot where B.D. usually sat. Bubba Two joined her, hands folded self-conscientiously on his lap.

"I came over to see you."

"OK. Now you've seen me." She pretended to get up.

"Hey, don't leave yet. I want you to go jet skiing with me. Ever been?"

"Nope. Never been on a jet ski, but it sounds like fun."

"Oh, it is. It's really cool. It's like riding a motorcycle on the water. Those things go fast, I mean fast! It is like skimming over the top of the water, like a sea bird."

"Are they dangerous?" she asked.

"Only if you don't pay attention to what you are doing. No sharp turns and no showboating. Got to watch out for the bigger boats, too. Sometimes they don't look where they are going and you could get run over."

"When did you want to go jet skiing? Arianna asked.

"How about right now?"

"Do I need to take anything?"

"Wear a bathing suit or clothes that can get wet. Also, some water shoes in case you have to wade around where there are shells like oysters."

The two teenagers walked out onto the dock behind Bubba Two's family home. The twin jet skis were in the water, fueled up and ready to go. They looked very sleek, shiny, modern, floating there, electric blue, Yamaha 4-stroke Wave Runners, born to ride. One ski had a dive tank, regulator, BCD, and a pair of diving masks strapped to the rear seat with bungees.

"Here. Put this on." He handed Arianna a compact vest with a fat zipper and a whistle attached. "In case you fall overboard," he told her. She slipped into the life preserver, adjusted the straps, and zipped it up. She tested the whistle.

"If I need help, I use the whistle," she said to him. "I just pucker up and blow."

Bubba Two laughed. "Yep, just like Bogie in *To Have and Have Not*. Hop on the ski, Bacall. I'll show you how all this works."

Arianna settled onto the slick, upholstered vinyl seat. Bubba Two attached a stretchy, orange coiled wire around her wrist and plugged its black plastic clip into a slot on the steering handle. "If you fall off, this clip pulls out and idles the motor. Push that little green button." The engine started immediately. "Use your finger to pull this metal hook. It's the throttle. The black button is the kill switch. See the high stream of water coming out the back? Keep an eye on that. It means that water is passing through the engine and keeping it cool. If you don't see that stream, shut down and check the water intake."

Bubba Two dropped expertly onto the molded seat on the other electric blue Yamaha. He hooked up the orange safety line and started his engine. "Follow me." He pointed the jet ski nose out into the Kitchen and slowly turned left, to the east. Arianna watched his stream of water shoot from the ski then checked to see that hers was working. Bubba Two dropped back alongside Arianna and shouted, "We are going to go over to Palma Sola Bay and get you checked out on this new machine. Then we'll scoot across Tampa Bay, take a close-up look at the Sunshine Skyway, check out the lighthouse, inspect the old gun emplacement at Fort DeSoto, scuba-dive off Egmont Key, then take in a little sun. Sound good to you?"

"Sounds good to me," she nodded back, over the humming sound of the pair of high-performance, four-cylinder engines. Bubba touched his throttle and spurted into the lead. Arianna followed. They maintained careful control as they went under the bridge at Manatee Avenue and entered a large lagoon-like body of water. "This is a good place for you to try out your jet ski. There is no one around. See what kind of speed you feel comfortable with. Remember, no sudden moves. You could be tossed and I can tell you from experience, water is very hard and unyielding when hit at high speed. Go."

Arianna slowly squeezed the hook-like throttle and the shiny, electric blue ski jumped ahead, faster than she expected. She kept control and increased her speed. She slewed to the right and then to the left, did several figure eights, then made a wide circle and headed back in the other direction, all the way to shore. She looked around. She checked the rear-view mirror and the stream of cooling water. The only other vessel in the secluded area was Bubba Two's jet ski, over near the bridge. She flew the full length of the inlet at full throttle, 40 miles per hour. The wind wrinkled her face, whipped her eyelashes, blew her mouth open and filled it with rushing air. She squinted tight. "This is exciting!" she said to herself, "I've never gone so fast before, but I sure need some goggles." She slowed at the other shore and made a u-turn. She slewed into fast-throttle figure eights, left, then right, then left, over the trace of her wake, forming the double circles of the number eight. As she went even faster in a sharp turn, she found herself skipping across the water like a flat stone, the drag tugged her bathing suit bottom sharply against her body. Salt water spewed into her mouth. She coughed and struggled for air as she came to a final stop. The life preserver kept her at the surface.

Bubba Two came alongside, guiding her idling jet ski with one arm. "You OK?"

"Yep. The water does hurt! Like you said, it's hard." She climbed back on her ski. "I'm ready for Tampa Bay." She sped away under the narrow Manatee Avenue Bridge leading out of the lagoon, water spurting proudly from the engine. Bubba Two picked up the lead and the electric blue jet skis passed along the old fishing village of DeSoto, then turned north around Price's Key and under the Manatee Avenue drawbridge connecting to Anna Maria Island. They navigated at minimum wake speeds through the Intracoastal Waterway, the ICW, turning west at Gilligan's Island, the spoil left over from deepening the channel.

Bubba Two dropped alongside Arianna, "Let's make a quick run over to the Sunshine Skyway. It looks very different from the water. Big. Tall." He zipped ahead. Arianna maintained pace as the jet skis barely touched the water on the way to the massive bridge at top speed. "I feel like a Hell's Angels mermaid!" she repeated over and over to herself, amazed at the freedom of racing inches above the water.

They approached the south fishing pier and slowed to a crawl, maintaining distance from the casting fishermen above. "This is what's left of the old Skyway. You can see the two roadways. The one on the far side was the first bridge, just two lanes. Then the second bridge, a twin of the first, was built. The old bridge was then used for northbound traffic and the new bridge was used for southbound traffic. It was a miracle to be able to cross Tampa Bay by car, after centuries of boat traffic, first by the various Indian tribes, then by

DeSoto, later the Cuban fishing camps, then the Florida pioneers, our people." Bubba Two pointed to the north. "The other fishing pier is way over there. It is the other end of the twin roadways and now is just used for fishing, like the one here. The two ends were left for people to enjoy the outdoors after the center sections were torn down and hauled away."

"Torn down?" Arianna asked. "What for?"

"A freighter, the Summit Venture, hit a support column of the southbound bridge and knocked the center span down onto the bow of the ship and into the water. Killed a lot of people. A real tragedy. Cars just kept falling from the sky, then a Greyhound Bus."

"That's terrible! How could something like that happen?"

"It was people, layers and layers of well-intentioned people. They did not want anything like that to happen. No one did. But it did happen. The channel was wide enough. The center span was as long as 4 football fields. The height under the bridge was the same as a 15-story building, able to handle the really big ships passing in and out of Port Tampa. The twin bridges were designed to stand forever. They could never fall on their own. Every single freighter going in and out was boarded and guided by a highly trained, licensed, experienced harbor pilot who knew Tampa Bay like it was his own back yard. The assigned pilots directed everything from the ship's bridge. They were on watch, on duty, on alert. It was just another humdrum, wet, misty morning in May 1980, people going to work. What could go wrong?"

"If everybody was so sure this could never happen, what went wrong?" Arianna posed the question to Bubba Two as they floated together off the fishing pier.

"Bad things came together, all at once. It was early morning, around first light, a hard rain. It was not just another humdrum, wet, misty morning in May. Witnesses said there was a torrential monsoon, raining cats and dogs. Motorists said their wipers could not keep up with the rain and they were blinded. Even with the pilot on duty in the wheel house, the freighter went off course and shattered a major support column. I've seen photos. The concrete was gone, sheared right off. The center span fell onto the bow of the ship and into Tampa Bay. Cars kept right on driving in the downpour and fell into the water. Then the bus went over. A lot of people died, more than 30." Bubba Two sat silent on his jet ski, an out-stretched leg holding Arianna's ski alongside.

Arianna stared into the water. "I guess the channel was wide, but not wide enough. The pilot knew Tampa Bay like his own back yard, but couldn't see out the windows of the wheel house in the heavy downpour. Sounds like a good example of Murphy's First Law: *Anything that can go wrong, will go wrong.*"

"And, you are right," Bubba Two reacted. "Looking back, there were things that should have been done but were not done. All freighter traffic should have been halted until the weather cleared. There should have been protection built in for the support columns. Hey, let's take a look at the new bridge and you can see how changes were made to prevent anything like that from ever happening again." He led the way north to the center span of the Sunshine Skyway.

Arianna looked up as they flew over the water running right alongside the world-famous bridge. From down below, the Skyway took on gigantic dimensions, much more so than crossing in a car overhead. The architectural lines were clean and delicate, while the mass and the strength of the structure displayed itself. The long center span was held up with bright yellow cables dropping down to the center of the roadbed.

"What are all these big round things sticking up out of the water?" she asked him.

"Dolphins," he responded.

"Dolphins?"

"Yep. That's what the engineers call them. They are placed in such a way as to make the support columns unapproachable. Any freighter off course will hit these dolphins, but not the bridge. One less thing to go wrong."

"Yeah, well, have you ever heard of Murphy's Corollary 4?"

"No. Tell me. I know you are dying to tell me."

"I am," she huffed. "Murphy also told us, *If you perceive that there are four possible ways in which something can go wrong, and circumvent these, then a fifth way, unprepared for, will promptly develop.* "

"Where do you get all this stuff?"

"I read a lot," she stared at him, "and I remember what I read."

"Well, did you notice that there are hundreds and hundreds of tons of concrete in these protective dolphins? And you are a big reader, so you know about the disappearance of the head of the Teamsters' Union, Jimmy Hoffa, and you know his body has never been found. Well, Miss-Remember-What-You-Read, local legend has it that Jimmy Hoffa is on guard right here, protecting the Sunshine Skyway, entombed forever in one of these dolphins. I read a lot, too."

Arianna floated idly on her jet ski. She could see the order and discipline of the placement of the dolphins and recognized that the bridge supports were protected from freighters. "Hah, the next thing," she thought mischievously, "Murphy's *fifth way* will promptly develop, a freighter will hit a dolphin, sink in the channel, and block all ship traffic for weeks." She bent her head back all the way to look up at the roadway far above. "Awesome," she mumbled, "Never saw anything so big, so up close."

Bubba Two came alongside and stretched his leg out to hold them together. He pointed to the west. "See that low land over there? Keep an eye on the north end, off to the right. Look for the light to blink."

Arianna saw the light blink and barely made out a white lighthouse. "Oh," she said, "I saw that beacon from Emerson Point."

Bubba Two pressed his finger down on the throttle and raced away, yelling, "Let's head over to the lighthouse on Egmont Key!" His jet ski spurted a high stream of water into the air as he peeled away.

CHAPTER 11
FORT DESOTO

Arianna kept up with Bubba Two as they buzzed toward the lighthouse on Egmont Key, both at full throttle for the long run across Tampa Bay. She used every sense of awareness to keep her partner in the corner of her eye and to control the powerful jet ski under her as it took on its own life and performed as it was designed - fast, nimble, responsive, thrilling, perilous. She maintained a bee line to avoid being thrown from the seat as happened in the lagoon when she was learning to ride. She checked for other water craft, aware that she was riding low on the water and might not be seen by taller boats. She looked back through the mirror and confirmed that the cooling water was spurting high into the air. Off to the right, she saw a freighter moving steadily along the channel on its way to the Gulf of Mexico and on to mysterious foreign ports around the world. She lived the moment, wanting it to last, hurtling across the bay, her pony tail fluttering, her eyes squinting.

Bubba Two slowed down and floated just offshore. Arianna came alongside. He held her there with an outstretched leg on her ski. "That's Egmont Key. The lighthouse has been there a very long time. That freighter we passed back there is like the one that hit the Skyway. It is over 600 feet long, so you can get an idea of the power and force of these big ships. See the launch drawing up to the side of the big ship? It will pick up the pilot and take him back over to the pilot station." He pointed to a large dock and buildings to the south of where they were. "The launch takes a pilot out to each ship when it comes in and then picks up the pilot when a ship goes out. I know one thing I'll bet you don't know. When your grandpa, Captain B.D. Bradford, was born back in the 1930's his daddy ran the pilot launch here on Egmont. That's some family history for you."

A rush of pride came to Arianna as she realized that her forebears lived and worked where she now sat on the jet ski, that her great grandfather used his skills every day to make a living on the water, operating the launch that ferried pilots to the big ships inbound and picked them up again on the way out.

"On that day when the freighter hit the bridge, did the launch take the pilot out?"

"Yes. For sure. Right where we are now. That's the way it has been done from the very start when the ship channel was dug for Port Tampa all those years ago. And it's just the same today as it was then." He pointed to a long stretch of white sand to the north on the far side of the ship channel. "That's Mullet Key. Over a hundred years ago, the government built Fort DeSoto there. It was around 1899, during the Spanish-American War."

"You really do read, don't you! You told me about that when we were fishing. You said you would take me over there. Tell me more about the war."

"Well, the USS Maine was docked in Havana Harbor in Cuba, a Spanish colony at the time. It blew up, tied there at the dock. It was in every newspaper in the world. Headlines screamed 'Sabotage!' Many Americans blamed the Cubans and called for revenge, shouting, 'Remember the Maine'. And that's what started the Spanish-American War."

"Then what?"

"Oh, people got all worked up and had night-mares about the Spanish Armada sailing into American ports and attacking our homeland. The evidence is right here in this area. Remember the huge slabs of concrete we passed when we were sardine fishing?"

"Yes, I do. It was quite a pile of concrete slabs out in the water."

"Well, that was one of the gun emplacements built to protect Tampa Bay from the Armada. The big slabs were at the south end of Egmont, on the other side of where we are currently. There was another gun emplacement at the north end of Egmont, just beyond the lighthouse. Some of it is still there. Two gun emplacements were built on Mullet Key as well as barracks for troops which came to be called Fort DeSoto. One emplacement washed away from the many storms over the years, but there is one emplacement preserved in place with the big guns still there. The barracks are still there, too."

"Did the Spanish Armada ever show up?"

"Not a chance. There was never even a threat. Angry Americans demanded forts, the War Department gave them forts. They demanded shore batteries for protection, they got shore batteries. "

"How did the war end up?"

"It was over about the time it started. As war reparations, Spain gave us Cuba, Puerto Rico, and the Philippines. A few years later, the US relinquished all claims to Cuba and helped it become an independent nation. Then the Philippines were also freed and gained independence. The US still has Puerto Rico, which may someday become our 51st state."

"You sure know a lot about history."

"Yep, thanks to Manatee High School. I keep my nose in the books."

"And your brother, Bubba One?"

"Yep, him, too, but he doesn't want anyone to know he makes good grades. He says he has a reputation to maintain. Let's go inspect Fort DeSoto." He slowly removed his leg to release her ski. His foot caught the back of Arianna's calf. She was surprised at the tingle that rippled through her. She wondered if he touched her by accident. Bubba Two gunned his jet ski and flew north across the ship channel toward the west end of Mullet Key.

Bubba Two pulled the jet skis partly onto the sandy beach. He removed dock line and small anchors from the bow hatches of the two skis and pushed the flukes into the sand to hold the boats in place. They dropped their vests over the watercraft handlebars. He led the way along a sandy path among sea oats and small dunes. One large dune rose off to their right.

"Is that an Indian shell mound?" Arianna asked.

"Gun emplacement," he replied. "The Army Corps of Engineers poured thick concrete walls and then piled tons and tons of sand in front for protection. I'll show you how it all works. I've been here before."

When they were past the high dune, Arianna saw the large, flat expanse that was once an active Army post, Fort DeSoto. They inspected the gun emplacement. It was a large, open, roofless square with a concrete floor and three tall, thick concrete walls. There were two gigantic weapons designed to blow up and sink enemy ships approaching Tampa Bay.

"These are 12-inch mortars," Bubba Two explained. They stood next to the long-abandoned weapons, taller than they were. "The gunners must have had some kind of trolley to haul the powder and the projectiles from the storeroom, so they could load the mortars and fire them. These are Model 1890-M1. Each mortar weighs 138,000 pounds. The explosive charge weighed 65 pounds and could blow through 6" steel plating six miles at sea. These emplacements are called gun pits. This one is named Battery Laidley after a decorated Army colonel."

Arianna stared at Bubba Two in disbelief. "How could you know all that? I don't care about your straight A's in history, no one can know all that. Battery Laidley, indeed! Hah! Did you just make it up?"

"No, I did not make it up. I read the historical marker right over there." He pointed to a mounted plaque to prove his point.

Arianna looked around. All she could see in three directions was concrete rising up high. The emplacement was open to the rear. Bubba Two looked around. "How could they aim?" he asked. "They can't see a thing. How would they know if they even hit the target?"

"They posted spotters in towers," Arianna explained to him, expressionless and matter-of-fact. "They had powerful binoculars and relayed information to the data booths right behind the gun pits. They talked over wire-line telephones. There were no walkie-talkies back then. Communicating back and forth with the spotters, the data booths computed new settings and relayed those instructions to the gun crews with slate boards. The crews adjusted the mortars and were able to zero in on the targets, even though the ships were moving in the water. These mortars fired huge explosive charges high into the air, and then they dropped down onto the target. The sand dune in front would protect them from the big naval weapons carried on ships. Naval weapons are guns, not artillery. Those guns fire straight at targets such as other ships or ground-based forts. That's why there is no roof on this emplacement and it is open to the rear. Naval guns can hit the sand dune in front, but any other shots just fly over. The ships guns can't reach down here where the defensive weapons are placed in defilade."

Bubba Two was slack jawed, breathing through his mouth. "Slate boards, indeed! Hah! Did you just make it up?"

"No, I did not make it up. I read the historical marker right over there." She pointed to a mounted plaque.

CHAPTER 12
EGMONT KEY

They zipped up their life vests, picked up the anchors, and pushed the jet skis into knee-deep water, then washed the sand off the small anchors and stowed them back in the forward hatches. Bubba Two led the way back across the ship channel to the Gulf of Mexico side of Egmont Key. They rode very slow along the beach and Arianna admired the shoreline and palms, recognizing that hundreds, even thousands, of years ago people lived there, and life among the Indians had many benefits. She felt an urge to build a palm-thatched hut on Egmont and cook over an open fire, even though the signs along the beach declared it to be a bird sanctuary, not open for camping.

They motored to the south end, up to the great slabs of concrete piled together away from the beach. Bubba Two dropped into the water and released the anchor from the forward hatch. He tied Arianna's ski to his and displayed a red diver's flag with a white diagonal stripe. The two boats floated together anchored next to the jumbled structure.

"Take off your life vest," he said and hopped up on her ski behind her. He removed the scuba diving gear from his ski and arranged it behind her back. "Put this on." She slipped her arms through the weighted BCD as he balanced the heavy tank and turned on the air flow. "Fasten the Velcro straps good and tight across the front." He reached the mouthpiece of the respirator over to her face and held it so she could see. "This is what you breathe through. See how it fits inside your mouth? Bite down. Always blow into it when you first put it in your mouth to clear any water inside. Then you take normal breaths, in and out, slow. Give it a try." She inserted the mouthpiece and blew. A small amount of water shot out. She took several slow breaths then removed it. "Hey, this works. I can breathe just fine. Can I get in the water?"

"Not just yet. The vest you are wearing is called a BCD. That stands for Buoyancy Control Device. You can inflate it to rise and float. He held her finger over a button and pushed. She heard the air flow and felt the vest squeeze her body as it inflated. "Then, if you want to sink and dive, you push this button." He pushed her finger on the button to deflate the device.

"I got it. I'm ready."

"Not just yet. Inflate the vest." She pushed the button until she felt the pressure against her upper body. "OK, get in the water, real slow." Bubba Two held the loop at the back of the vest as she entered the water, just in case. She floated safely and he let go. "Now, here's the mask. Wet it, spit in it. Wipe the spit around the glass, rinse it out, then put it on. Make sure it fits just right and no water can get in." She followed his instructions and fitted the mask, all spitted and rinsed. The glass covered her eyes like goggles. Below that, the thin plastic of the mask followed the shape of her nose.

"What's the spit for? Good luck?"

"Nope. Helps keep the glass from fogging up. Now I want you to sink until your head is barely underwater. Stay right at that level. Relax. Get comfortable. Breathe normally. Look around. Then inflate to come back up and float on the surface."

Bubba Two watched the top of Arianna's head as she floated suspended just below the surface.

She pushed the inflate button and rose up, removing the regulator and taking the mask off. "That's great. You can really see. It's a whole different world under water."

"Now, this time I want you to go all the way to the bottom. Just sit there and look around. It is only 10 to 15 feet deep, but if you feel any pressure on your ears, pinch your nose through the mask and blow gently. The rule in diving is to equalize early and often."

Arianna spit in her mask, smeared it around the glass, rinsed it out and put it on. She bit the regulator, blew out, pushed the deflate button, and sank slowly to the sandy bottom. She crossed her legs and sat there. It was a quiet world. She heard the air sounds of the scuba gear and was certain she heard her heart beating and stuff squishing inside her body. She watched the fish swim all around her, small and not so small, long and round, all with different eyes and colors, and fin shapes. The concrete slabs were only feet away, forming a great barrier. She was surprised to see Bubba Two swim up to her, wearing the second mask. He reached behind her and put a regulator in his mouth, then locked his legs around her body to keep from floating away. He pointed to the fish and the concrete and gave her a thumbs-up. Arianna felt a sense of comfort and security, a tingle of excitement. For the first time in her life, she sat on a sandy ocean bottom, breathing comfortably under water, observing the sea around her, embraced by a sensitive and caring person. Life among the fish had many benefits. She wanted to explore the underwater world from now on.

They sat there a long time. It was a good place to be. Arianna felt warm and protected. Bubba Two showed her the air gauge. They still had plenty of air, but the needle was moving toward the red. He pointed up. She pushed the inflate button and they rose together.

Bubba Two used the bungees to stow the dive gear on the back of his jet ski. He put away the dive flag. They sat on the skis, relaxed in the sunshine, taking in the clean, salty sea air. "That was great," she told him. "Water is a whole different dimension. I want to do this again. Say, where did that second regulator come from? I did not know it was there."

"It's called an octopus. It's bright yellow, so it's easy to find in deep water. It is a safety feature, so if another diver gets low on air, or runs out, or has some kind of breathing problem, the octopus is there for emergencies. Very handy, smart to have."

"I really like being under the water," she gushed. "It's a new dimension to living. Someday I want to learn to fly and discover that dimension, too. Life is fun!"

"Beach time," Bubba Two announced. He untied Arianna's ski and lifted the anchor. They motored to shore and pulled the bows of the skis up onto the beach and buried the anchor flukes in the sand. He removed two large towels from the hatch, along with a plastic bottle of suntan oil. They stretched out on the towels on the white, sandy beach and enjoyed the tropical Florida afternoon.

The sun warmed her body. She felt the skin shrink on her face from the sun and the salt water. She sat up and squeezed oil into her palms and spread it onto her forehead and cheeks, down her neck, over her arms and legs. She looked at Bubba Two lying face down on his towel, lost to the world. She turned the plastic container upside down and squirted up and down from his neck to his waist. "Hey, what's going on?" he grumbled.

"Just a little sun tan oil sending you a message."

"Message?"

"Yeah. I just wrote 'BB2' in oil. That's your name isn't it?" She rubbed the oil around on his back, pushing hard against the muscles.

"Hey, that feels good," Bubba said. She put oil on his arms and legs and massaged it into the skin.

"Your turn." She handed him the container.

He squeezed up and down on her back and rubbed the oil in.

"What did you write?"

"It's personal."

"C'mon! What did you write?"

"Eye-el-oh-vee-ee-y-oh-u."

Arianna's ears buzzed and a tingle rippled through her body. She sat up and looked at Bubba Two, his face red from the sun. Or. . . ?

It was time to go, Arianna knew, before things got out of hand.

Just south of Egmont, riding back to DeSoto on the jet skis, Bubba Two pulled alongside Arianna and motioned for her to slow down. As they floated, he pointed out in the distance several sandbars showing above the low tide. Sea birds were everywhere. Several boats were anchored off the sandbars on the bay side protected from the surf. "Remember Passage Key? This is all the same as it was 500 years ago when the Spanish first came to this part of the world. That's Anna Maria Island there to the south. You can see Bean's Point. Tampa Bay was written about by those early explorers. Some called it the Bay of Tocobaga after the Indian tribe that lived at what we now know as Safety Harbor at the top of Old Tampa Bay. DeSoto called it Bahia de Espiritu de Santo, the Bay of the Holy Spirit. These sandbars were right here back then. I ran across a description of them written long ago by a man named Juan Lopez de Velasco. He said the entrance to Tampa Bay had *three little islets in it on which there is nothing at all except sand and birds*. That's Passage Key!"

Arianna was very impressed with Bubba Two's deep-seated connection with the culture and history of Florida. She grinned at him and asked, "Heh! Where's the historical marker you're reading from?"

"Right here in my head," he tapped his temple. "Oh, one more thing," Bubba Two snickered impishly, "DeSoto would turn over in his watery grave if he knew that Passage Key is now the local nude beach. Wanna go over there?"

Without a word or a glance, Arianna squeezed her throttle and sped away.

CHAPTER 13
FISHING IS DANGEROUS WORK

"Hey, wait for me!" Bubba One yelled as he ran down the dock and leaped out onto the net piled high at the stern of the Six Js. The other crew members paid him no attention as he hunkered down on the net. "You could of waited a minute or two! What's the big hurry?" He pouted as the other crew members busied themselves readying the rig for fishing. The bait boat turned south after passing Price's Key and motored under the Cortez Bridge. Arianna, dressed in her orange oilers, white boots, and crew cap sat in the wheelhouse with Hands and Bubba Two as Cap'n Joe Mac steered under the Longboat Key Bridge and through the pass into the Gulf of Mexico. They approached the Longboat Pass channel marker sticking up high above the water, displaying the letters *LP*. Cap'n Joe Mac slid the side window open and tossed a handful of coins into the water. Hands reached in the pocket of his cut-off jeans, held up with a length of rope, which also kept his fish knife, ever sheathed at his side. He tossed several coins out the window. Bubba Two took a dollar bill out of his wallet and threw it overboard. "Got no change," he muttered.

"Just wasting good money!" They heard Bubba One scream from the net.

"What was that all about?" Arianna asked.

Cap'n Joe Mac smiled. "Bubba One just isn't part of our crew. Tossing the coins out is what all the fishermen do when they go out Longboat Pass. It's supposed to bring you good luck and get you back home. The old story is that if you can see the Longboat Pass marker, you can swim the rest of the way home, even if the boat sinks." Arianna found several coins in her cut-offs and threw them out the window, saying, "Here's to a safe return." The four people in the wheelhouse nodded. They settled themselves for the ride out to fishing depth and took in the fresh, clean Gulf air, the Florida sunshine, and the ocean views.

"How far out do we fish? Arianna asked.

"We can fish out to where the net still reaches the bottom, otherwise the fish will just swim under the lead line. We have to be at least three miles from shore," Hands told her. "That's another one of those made-up rules."

"Made-up rules?"

"Yep. Us fishermen have had to live with made-up rules as long as we've been on the water. Years ago, the powers-that-be banned stop-netting which made it harder to fish and make a living. Then they set up open seasons and closed seasons for mullet, then for stone crabs, then for lobster. Then they made it a serious crime to have even one stone crab claw on the boat under 2 and 3/4 inches, even if it was for your own supper. Had to throw good food overboard or go to jail. Next they forced long-line grouper boats to get a special permit to fish and to stay offshore in water at least 20 fathoms deep, then lately only certain boats were allowed to use long-line gear at all. Offshore boats had to get special hook removers in case they got a sea turtle, plus a huge net and pole to bring them on deck to free them, plus a spare tire so the turtle would not be forced to lie flat on the deck. Couldn't keep any grouper under 20 inches. Perfectly edible, marketable fish were thrown overboard. Had to get special hollow needles to push into the stomach of these so-called undersized cadet grouper to let out air from the change in pressure coming up from the bottom. They told us that by releasing the air pressure, the discarded fish would swim back to the bottom. What actually happened is that the porpoises started following grouper boats and getting free meals. I have watched it day in and day out where the grouper were de-hooked, depressurized, tossed back in the water, and degested by the waiting porpoises. Chomped right down in one gulp. Not only that, the porpoises started robbing the long lines set along the bottom by pulling caught fish off the hook and eating them up. Porpoises are plenty smart. They know how to avoid hooks.

"The powers-that-be forced offshore grouper boats to have a VMS, a Vessel Monitoring System, so they could track their whereabouts. Whether they fished or not, the boats also had to pay a high monthly fee for the VMS so the government could track them. The captains were observing the rules and there were very few violations, but the complex and expensive VMS system was forced on us. The government is really good at regulating problems that do not exist. Next thing you know, every boat is hit with an IFQ, Individual Fishing Quota, and could only catch a certain number of fish. Many a boat would fill their IFQ then sit idle for weeks. I liked the old way of fishing. If you could take the risk, put together a boat, fishing gear, and a crew, then go out and find fish and get them on the boat, you made a living. Nowadays, it takes an administrative genius to assemble all the permits, a well-heeled banker to pay all the fees, and a law school graduate to know and obey all the made-up rules. Now you even have to notify the NMFS, National Marine Fisheries Service, when you go out and when you come in. It's like giving machine guns to children. Truth is, you'll be lucky if you don't get put in jail and fined for breaking a made-up rule. It just ain't fair. All us fishermen have been criminalized."

Cap'n Joe Mac and Bubba Two remained quiet, hearing Hands ventilate and rant about regulating the fishing industry. They had heard it all before.

"That's terrible!" Arianna uttered in disbelief. "Terrible? You ain't heard nothin' yet!" Hands sputtered. "The fishermen have been regulated right out of business! Twenty years ago, the sports fishermen started a senseless campaign to ban net fishing. They spent millions of dollars to get rid of commercial net fishing. They wanted all the fish for themselves. They lied to the public over and over. They knew they were lying, we knew they were lying. When the vote came in, Florida banned net fishing. It just wasn't fair. The net opponents were careful not to mention that mullet is a vegetarian and will not bite a baited hook. It is not a sports fish, yet that is the one fish most affected by the net ban. Nowadays, we all get out on the water in the late fall when the roe mullet show up and do our best to catch them with cast nets we throw from skiffs. The cast nets are really small, under 14 feet, and it takes hundreds of throws to bring in enough fish to make it pay. The sports fishermen were just putting commercial fishermen out of business for no good reason. They had the money and they got their way."

Arianna looked back to the stern where the huge net was piled high. "We have a net. How can we fish legally?"

"Yeah, and that's part of the net ban story. Under the new rules, a net can only total 500 square feet. If you want a net 100 feet long, it can only have 5 feet of mesh, you know, webbing, from the cork line to the lead line. A net 50 feet long can have a depth of 10 feet, and so on. Can't do much with 500 square feet, no matter how it is configured, so we use cast nets and I can tell you, throwing cast nets is for strong, young men."

"Our net is bigger than 100 square feet."

"Yeah," Hands nodded. "After the nets were banned, the sports fishermen realized there wasn't any more bait for game fishing. The richy-riches shot themselves in the foot. So they went to Tallahassee and made it legal for bait boats to use nets. Naturally, we have to be at least 3 miles offshore so nobody can see us fishing.

"Believe me, commercial fishing is drawing its last breath. Even the fish house we work out of is putting pressure on fishermen. We never paid for ice. Now the owner is talking about charging us money. He's even threatened to bill us for tying our boats up. One day I expect to find parking meters installed all along the shore. Pretty soon they'll shut down the accounts we use to keep our gear in shape until we can catch some fish. Greed is gonna do us in, just wait and see."

"Fishfinder, Fishfinder, this is the Six Js, over."

"Got you loud and clear, Six Js," the pilot in the small spotter airplane responded. "Just off to the right, big school, might be the right stuff."

"We'll check it out. Six Js clear."

The crew went out on deck and checked to see that the boat was ready to made the strike and bring in the Spanish sardines. Cap'n Joe Mac eased into the black mass of fish and confirmed it to be the right stuff. He drove the boat up ahead and positioned it to take in the massive school with the net.

"Let 'er go!" he shouted to the crew.

Arianna watched as the net played out off the stern of the boat and unraveled when the weight of the lead line took it to the bottom and the corks arranged themselves in a bobbing row to hold up the net at the top of the water. The wall of net was in place as the boat returned to the start and the crew secured the circle, capturing the fish.

Hands and Bubba Two stood near the rail and looked down into the net full of flopping sardines. Bubba One joined them inspecting the catch.

"See any porpoises down there?" he asked with a sneer.

The other two crewmen ignored him and readied the tom weight to be dropped overboard to hold the net in place.

Squooloosh! The big 300-pound, half-dome of lead hit the water, the line screamed through the block overhead.

"Maybe there's sharks down there this time," Bubba One snickered. As he stepped away from the rail, he butted Bubba Two with this head. Trying to keep his balance, Bubba Two fell backward, his foot landed dead center in the blue cut-off plastic barrel as the tom weight uncoiled the line at high speed.

Arianna was horrified to see Bubba Two snatched like a rag doll from the deck, jerked into the air, his ankle wrapped in rope and jammed at the overhead block. The boat tipped slightly to the side as the tom weight caught and stopped, hanging in the water off the side of the boat. She saw Bubba Two's body hang from the block, his head and shoulders slumped against the deck. She cried out.

Bubba One screamed, "Oh, no!" He covered his face with his hands as tears of anguish and remorse welled up in his eyes.

Cap'n Joe Mac rushed from the wheelhouse with the first aid kit. Hands, quick as lightning, cut the tom weight line with his fishing knife. Arianna rushed to cradle Bubba Two's head. Hands, acting quickly, cut off the pants leg of the orange oilers and the white boot with his fishing knife. Blood pulsed in spurts from the wound. His leg was broken, a compound fracture, the tibia and fibula protruded through the skin. Hands pinched the pressure point near the top of the young man's thigh and held it firmly. Cap'n Joe Mac wrapped a tourniquet just below the injured man's knee and tightened it. The bleeding slowed. He placed a large sterile compress over the opening, inches above the ankle, to protect the wound. The bleeding stopped. Cap'n Joe Mac told Arianna to bring a pillow off the bunk in the wheelhouse. He placed it under and around the leg and taped it to hold the leg rigid. He removed the tourniquet.

Bubba One lay next to his twin, his head resting on his chest. "Oh, no, Bubba, oh, no, no, no. I'm sorry. I am so sorry. I love you, brother. Forgive me. I promise never to hurt you again. Just stay with us. Stay with us. I promise I will be a better person, a brother you can be proud of. I'm so sorry, Bubba."

"Coast Guard! Coast Guard! This is the Fishing Vessel Six Js calling the United States

Coast Guard. Come in, Coast Guard." Cap'n Joe Mac spoke into the VHF radio.

"This is the United States Coast Guard, Search and Rescue Station DeSoto. Go ahead Six Js."

"We have a seriously wounded crew member on board. His leg is broken, a compound fracture, and he lost a lot of blood. He needs immediate evacuation to Bayfront Medical Center. Over."

"What is your location, Six Js?"

"We are five miles west of Longboat Pass."

"Affirmative, Six Js. A Coast Guard cutter is underway to evacuate your crew member. Remain on Channel 16 for further instructions."

Cap'n Joe Mac inspected the wound. The bleeding was stanched. He replaced the sterile compress over the break with a fresh one. He taped it securely, recalling the first aid instructions he had memorized many years before, *Stop the bleeding, protect the wound, prevent shock*. Bubba Two was unconscious, pale, ashen, and grey from loss of blood. The captain told Arianna to stay with Bubba Two while he and the other crew members took in the net. The power block hauled the net back onto the stern, the fish released into the open water. They waited and soon saw the Coast Guard cutter approach.

The evacuation was over in minutes. The crew of the Coast Guard cutter had Bubba Two strapped to a flat stretcher, and transferred over to the cutter which was then underway to shore for a helicopter transfer to the Bayfront Medical Center in St. Petersberg.

The Six Js returned empty to port in the village of DeSoto, Cap'n Joe Mac grimly steering the boat in the wheel house. Bubba One sat on the net and was consoled by Arianna. "I love my brother," he told her over and over. "I have not been the brother to him that he deserved, but that's all changed. It's different now. I am going to make him proud. Even if he loses his foot, I'll show him he can count on me."

CHAPTER 14
A HARD NIGHT
AND A HARD DAY

Arianna tossed in bed. It was a hard night. She dreamed, bad things, good things, nightmares. She talked to herself. She hated Bubba One. She wanted all this to stop, just stop, roll the clock back and put everyone back on the deck of the Six Js, the crew all together, unharmed, in one piece.

Arianna watched as Bubba Two stood on the cork line supported by Hands to free the porpoise trapped in the net. He smiled back at her, pleased that he had helped the big fish to free itself and return to open water. She was proud of her new friend and his respect for innocent beings in nature.

She was in a state of blissful suspension sitting on the sandy bottom, looking at the many fish moving back and forth in front of the jumbled concrete walls of the old fort, now sunk below the sea. Bubba Two held onto her to keep from rising, breathing together from the scuba tank.

On the Egmont beach, she wrote BB2 *on his back with the suntan oil. She heard him repeat* eye-el-oh-vee-ee-y-oh-u *as he wrote on her back then massaged the oil into her skin.*

Arianna woke, frightened, gasping for breath, pushing hard against the mattress with her feet, gripping tight the arrow head on the leather thong around her neck.

She heard the rope singing through the block as the heavy, lead tom weight dropped furiously into the water to hold the end of the net and anchor the pursing line that ran through the stainless steel rings attached to the lead line. She knew fishing was dangerous work. She saw Bubba One angrily head butt his twin brother. She could not understand how Bubba Two could be snatched so quickly and easily when the line caught his foot. She saw his head strike the deck as his leg was drawn tight against the block and held there. Hands was like lightning with his fish knife held to his waist by the length of rope. He cut the tom weight loose and let Bubba Two gently down onto the deck.

She saw Cap'n Joe Mac rush from the wheelhouse with the first aid kit to attend to Bubba Two's injuries. Would the doctors have to amputate?

She wondered if Bubba Two lost too much blood to survive and if she would ever see him again when the Coast Guard moved him swiftly onto the cutter and roared away to get him to the trauma center.

She knew she could never be around Bubba One again. Never speak to him again. His behavior was so bad, so evil. He should never have *shoved his twin into the water when the porpoise was snared in the net. He should never have butted him with his head. Why couldn't Bubba One have <u>his</u> leg caught in the rope? It would serve him right for all the bad things he did.*

It was a hard night for Arianna. When she woke in a start and sat up in bed, she was surprised to see her grandfather, B.D. Bradford, sitting in a chair next to her.

"It's OK, my angel," he said as he took her hand and held it. "You need some down time. It's been a hard night and this will be a hard day for you, but we'll get through it. Whenever you think you can manage, we'll go over to Bayfront Medical Center in St. Petersberg and visit Bubba Two. I already checked in with the hospital. He is out of intensive care. He needed several blood transfusions. They saved his foot. No amputation. His bones were set and his leg is in a heavy cast. He can have visitors. You want to go see him?"

"Oh, yes, Pop! Let's go visit Bubba Two in the hospital."

The old 1939 Ford pickup truck labored as it started the climb up the rise of the Sunshine Skyway. B.D. shifted down to third gear and pressed the gas pedal. Arianna looked out at the water far below and the bright yellow cables up above. She remembered Bubba Two's story about the old bridge tumbling down when it was hit by a freighter over thirty years ago. She wished she were once again sitting on the jet ski listening to him sound as if he were reading from a historical marker.

They located the enormous trauma complex and found Bubba Two's room. He was asleep in the bed, his leg and cast hung from a harness in the ceiling. Bubba One sat in a chair beside the bed. He was asleep also, holding his twin brother's hand against his face. He sat up when Arianna and her grandfather entered.

His voice cracked as he saw them. "He's OK. His leg has been set. He should be back fishing in a few months. Doc said it might take a little longer to learn to walk without a limp." He stood up to make room for the visitors. Bubba Two woke up.

"Hey, great to see you guys. Glad you could make it over here."

Arianna approached the bed and gave him a warm hug and kissed his cheek. She sat in the chair next to the bed, blushing.

"I was so worried about you. I rolled and tossed all night. It is so good to see you are going to be all right again soon."

There was not much to say that made sense, so they all sat there, self-conscious, quiet, feeling the need to just be together and not say anything.

On the road back, Arianna said. "It was such a relief to see him and know that he will be back on his feet real soon. I mean really be back on his feet, both of them. I was so worried. Even Bubba One was worried. He's seems to be a different person now, not so mean. The nurse said he will not leave his brother's side, that he sleeps in the chair, then spends the whole day talking to him, saying how he is going to be a better brother, a true brother, his best friend."

"You know, Arianna," her grandfather said. "There are times when it takes something bad like this to happen to make something good come about. I think Bubba One is becoming a different person, a better person, someone people will enjoy being around."

The shiny, old blue truck needed to be dropped into third gear to make the rise up the Sunshine Skyway. Arianna enjoyed the open air and wide ocean as they traveled back to the old fishing village of DeSoto.

CHAPTER 15
SPECIAL DAY ON WALLY'S DOCK

Arianna took to her bed for the rest of the day and managed to survive through another hard night, but knowing Bubba Two was going to be all right relieved the stress. It was first light when she heard the now familiar chiming of the antique clock. She smelled the odor of coffee coming from the kitchen. Pouring a cup, she joined Pop to sit on the back steps.

"Darling," B.D. said to his granddaughter. "You've had a bad time of it. I wish your stay here would have been trouble free, but that's just not the way things always turn out. Bubba Two is going to be fine and I believe we will see a new person in Bubba One."

"I think you are right, Pop," she said as she sipped her coffee and took in the now familiar surroundings, the royal palms, the Alvah Taylor house, the silver palms sheltering the front yard, the red chimney at the house to the north, the four door shed, the blue truck.

"Well, this is a special day. And I have a special treat for you. Did Nathan ever mention Cousin Wally and his dock?"

"Oh, yes! He said I had to see it and if food was being served be sure to try it all. He mentioned raw oysters, barbequed mullet, and swamp cabbage. Said it was like eating local history."

"Well, today you get to meet Cousin Wally and visit his dock. We are getting together just before sunset. Now, let me swear you to secrecy."

B.D. told her about Cousin Wally and recent events. "For many years, Wally lived alone at his house on the shore and spent his days on the dock fishing with a hook and line, eating what he caught, sleeping in the hammock, and reading big, thick books. You could always find him on the dock. He lost his wife long ago and his daughters are grown and on their own. He just turned 70 and was able to live his life in the village without worrying about making a house payment or a car payment. Then he met Margie. I never saw a guy change so much so fast. He started acting like a teenager, smiling and joking, really enjoying every day. People noticed the change and soon learned about his new friend, Margie. They wished him well and congratulated him on his good fortune. He did not spend as much time on the dock anymore."

"Good for Cousin Wally," Arianna said, "and good for Margie for making him so happy."

"She's pretty happy herself," B.D. observed. "It is not easy for a woman to find a good man like Wally. They make a fine pair."

"So, I get to meet Cousin Wally and Margie at the dock this evening. That's great. It really will be a special day."

"More special than you think." B.D. laughed. "Wally proposed to Margie and she said yes. It is a big secret. They are getting married at sunset on Wally's dock. He asked me to be his best man."

Arianna squealed, "E-e-e-e! I can't wait. This is kind of like eloping but staying home. I can't wait. I can't wait."

B.D. and Arianna walked down the long connecting walkway over the water to get to the large covered dock. Wally and Margie hovered around the table laid out with snacks while a few friends and relatives congratulated them and wished them well. Everyone there, including the bride and groom wore tee shirts with three mullet fish and the words *Proud to Be a DeSoto Kid.*

"Oh, Arianna," Wally grinned, "it is so good to meet you. Your cousin, Nathan, was here at Thanksgiving when we had quite a feast. Sorry about the food today. All we have are a few snacks, but we tried to keep this real quiet. Otherwise, the whole village would show up and the dock couldn't handle all those people. We wanted to keep it small, just close family and a few friends."

Arianna took a shucked raw oyster on its shell off the table and splashed hot sauce on it. "Over the lips, past the tongue, look out stomach, here it come," she recited to B.D., repeating what he had said to Nathan when he was there in November. She gulped down her first raw oyster. Arianna's eyes watered. B.D. gave her a warm hug. She reached for another oyster, doused it with hot sauce and held it out for her grandfather to eat.

"Don't forget your tee shirts," Margie said, pointing to a table with various sizes stacked up for the wedding guests. "Everybody has to wear one, even the preacher." Arianna and B.D. pulled their tees on over the clothes they wore.

B.D. asked Wally, "Whose idea was it to elope to get married? I mean, a hundred yards from home, all the way to the dock."

"Oh," he said, "It was Margie's idea. We agreed to get married real quiet like, so eloping was the best choice. I told her I always wanted to elope to Las Vegas and get hitched at one of those drive through wedding chapels. It was hard to keep a straight face when I said I wanted an Elvis impersonator to sing *Blue Suede Shoes* while we sat in the rental car, said 'I do' and kissed like newlyweds."

Cousin Wally smirked as B.D. roared with laughter.

"Whose idea was it to wear the tee shirts?"

"Margie's," Cousin Wally answered. "She loves it here."

As the sun lowered in the western sky, people began to assemble for the ceremony. The minister positioned himself on the west side of the dock, looking away from the sun. Wally and Margie moved over to face him and the sunset.

"Hey, wait for us!"

Everyone looked up to see Bubba One running along the narrow walkway leading to the dock, pushing Bubba Two in a wheelchair at high speed, his cast stretched out in front.

"We heard about Cousin Wally and Margie eloping, even if everybody was sworn to secrecy. My brother and I weren't about to miss this," Bubba One reported.

"Yeah," Bubba Two chimed in. "We sweet-talked the nurses so they sweet-talked the doctors, so they let us go. Can't miss Wally and Margie's wedding on the dock. This is a special day!"

Arianna quickly secured two large shirts from the table. She handed a tee to Bubba One and helped Bubba Two into the other one. She dropped to her knees, hugged Bubba Two, and gave him a quick kiss on the lips. During the ceremony, she stood next to the wheel chair and held his hand. Bubba One was at her side. When she felt him take her other hand and squeeze it, she squeezed back.

The minister, resplendent in his DeSoto mullet tee, gathered everyone around and timed the service so that when Wally and Margie exchanged rings, said "I do," and gave one another a big smack, the sun dropped down in the western sky.

C H A P T E R 16
TPA TO SAN

A s they approached the short term parking area, B.D. pulled up to the machine and removed a parking ticket. The gate lifted and the truck wound its way up a circular concrete ramp to the open air parking on the roof of the terminal.

"I'm going to miss you," Arianna said hugging her grandfather as they stood at the parapet looking over toward Raymond James Stadium. The low and featureless panorama accentuated the sky, filled with silver-blue, lazy, bulky cumulus clouds. Water and land differed only in color. The tall buildings of downtown Tampa rose up to the south. St. Pete lay off to the right. The full expanse of Tampa Bay opened before them.

"I'm coming back, Pop," she said, as they approached Airside E. "I am just like Nathan." She pointed to the tee shirt she was wearing, *Proud to Be a DeSoto Kid*, then touched the bill of her cap with the embroidered logo of the Six Js and the word *crew* on the front.

"You'll be back. You have sand in your shoes. It's an old Florida saying. When you get sand in your shoes, you will always come back."

"Well," she smiled. "Both my shoes are full of sand."

"Good," her grandfather said, "now, let me give you a big ole Florida cracker hug."

Arianna entered the tram. She heard the speaker, "We are about to depart. Please stand clear of doors and hold handrail."

The tram moved silently out of the building and into brilliant sunshine. "We are arriving at Airside E serving domestic carriers with flights to major cities. Please exit through doors indicated by the green flashing light."

She passed through the check-in and proceeded along the igloo of the emplaning ramp into the airplane.

She could feel the release of the brakes and the increasing power of the jet engines. She was pulled back firmly in her seat by the thrust. The stubby light stanchions flashed by faster and faster and then dropped away from the airplane as it lifted gracefully from the grasping earth and rose into the freedom of the skies. She wrapped her fingers tight around the arrowhead hanging from the leather thong around her neck and said, "I really am proud to be a DeSoto kid."

CHAPTER 17
TWITTER

I n San Diego, Arianna received a Tweet from Bubba Two:

Went fishing yesterday. Bubba One tossed a five-dollar bill overboard as we passed the Longboat Pass channel marker. We miss you.

25826995R00104

Made in the USA
Charleston, SC
15 January 2014